WE WERE THERE
At the Driving of the
Golden Spike

"Come here," said a deep voice
by the window

WE WERE THERE
At the **Driving** of the **Golden Spike**

David Shepherd

Illustrated by
William K. Plummer

Dover Publications, Inc.
Mineola, New York

Bibliographical Note

This Dover edition, first published in 2013, is an unabridged republication of the work originally published in 1960 by Grosset and Dunlap, New York.

Library of Congress Cataloging-in-Publication Data

Shepherd, David, 1924–
 We were there at the driving of the golden spike / David Shepherd; illustrated by William K. Plummer.
 p. cm.
 "This Dover edition, first published in 2013, is an unabridged republication of the work originally published in 1969 by Grosset and Dunlap, New York.".
 Summary: "Travel back to the 1860s to witness the dramatic track-laying contest between the Union and Central Pacific Railroads as Irish immigrants Sheamus and Nora Cullen and their children travel westward by freight car and riverboat"—Provided by publisher.
 ISBN-13: 978-0-486-49259-9 (pbk.)
 ISBN-10: 0-486-49259-1
 [1. Railroads—United States—Fiction. 2. Voyages and travels—Fiction. 3. Immigrants—Fiction. 4. Irish Americans—Fiction. 5. Family life—Fiction.] I. Plummer, William K., illustrator. II. Title.

PZ7.S54365We 2013
[Fic]dc23

2013019137

Manufactured in the United States by LSC Communications
49259104   2017
www.doverpublications.com

Contents

Illustrations

WE WERE THERE

At the Driving of the
Golden Spike

CHAPTER ONE

A Fair Wage for a Young Lad

MIKE CULLEN stamped his feet on the cold cobblestones as he looked up at the fence. A man was writing on it with a piece of yellow chalk:

JOBS IN THE WEST

CALLAHAN CONSTRUCTION CO.

The man put the yellow chalk in his pocket and took out a green piece. He wrote:

SEE MR. RYAN AT *THE GREEN*.

"Are you Mr. Ryan?" asked Mike, his teeth chattering.

The man turned around. He had a broad red face that glowed in the cold.

"That's me," he said, smiling. One of his teeth, Mike saw, was gold.

"Do you have many signs to write?" the boy asked.

Mr. Ryan nodded.

"I'll write them for you," Mike offered eagerly. "I'll write them all over New York City. I'll work for a quarter a day."

Mr. Ryan laughed and said, "That's a fair wage for a young lad, but I'm not giving jobs writing signs. I'm giving jobs building the Union Pacific Railroad." He moved off along the fence under the bows of the clipper ships moored in the harbor beyond.

Mike walked up to the fence and looked through a crack at the harbor. The water was gray and misty. When he had left Ireland and crossed the Atlantic Ocean to America, only six months before, the sea had been green and warm.

He ran past Mr. Ryan, who had his chalk out again, and stopped in front of a warehouse. A sign read: "NO HELP WANTED." A man in a bowler hat was counting the crates that two boys unloaded from a cart. Mike tipped his cap. "Beggin' your pardon, sir. Any help wanted?" he inquired.

"Can't you read?" asked the man, jerking his thumb at the sign.

"Not very well, sir," said Mike. "But I'm strong as an ox, and I'm willing to work for—"

"Twenty-eight, twenty-nine, thirty," the man counted. The two boys, who had been staring at Mike, mumbled to each other in a foreign language and went on unloading the cart.

Mike ran on, sparks flying from the cleats on his shoes as his thin legs hopped over the cobblestones. His small, pointed nose was getting red in the cold.

"*Mach schnell!*" cried a voice above him. He brushed the brown hair out of his eyes and looked up. A boy was sitting on an anchor, painting the bow of a ship. He was about a year younger than Mike—perhaps thirteen.

"Need any help?" Mike called up.

"You paint ship? I go see New York? Sure." He flipped some paint off his brush at Mike.

"What will you pay me?" asked Mike.

The boy took off his red cap and scratched his head. His hair was so blond, it looked white. "A piece of old cheese," he said finally.

Mike laughed and ran on. But the thought of cheese made him feel hungrier. There would be nothing to eat in the house until his father came home with his week's pay. That wouldn't be before seven o'clock.

Mike stopped in the middle of a square. There was something familiar about the park on one side and the enormous stone castle on the other. Suddenly he recognized it: Castle Garden, the place where he and his family had first set foot in America. They had spent a whole day in the gloomy building waiting for officials to stamp their papers so they could pass through. The first man they had met outside had stolen two dollars from them . . .

"Hot knish! Potato knish!" An old man passed

hunched over a cart from which a fragrant steam trailed.

Mike called to him. "Going home? Can I push your cart home for you, mister?"

The pushcart vendor stopped. His leathery hand reached for a knish as he looked at Mike.

"Hot knish?" said the old man. Mike realized he didn't understand English.

"Give me seven!" said a voice behind Mike, as a man brushed past him and laid a dollar on the cart. "Bitter cold today," the man said, rubbing his hands. He had a stocky build and a squirrel face. Mike recognized him. It was the same man who had guided Mike's family to a boarding house the evening they got off the ship.

Mike reached for the man's shoulder. But he had slipped away through the crowd. Mike hurried after him.

When he caught up, the guide was passing out the knishes to an immigrant family. "And as soon as you get your land legs, I'll take you to your new home," he was saying in a friendly, authoritative way.

"You there!" Mike shouted. "You're the one took us to Magnolia Court six months ago, and my father gave you two dollars for the landlady, and you ran away."

"I've never seen you before in my life," said the squirrel-faced man.

"Give me back the two dollars!" Mike shouted.

"I make an honest living," said the man. People were beginning to gather about. "Now get out of here." He pushed Mike away roughly. The family began to talk excitedly together. Mike recognized the language as Yiddish.

"*Gonif!*" he said, pointing to the man. The family's father opened his eyes wide. "*Gonif!* Thief! *Gonif!*"

The father seized the guide by the arm. There was a flurry of excitement. The squirrel-faced man stopped grinning. He pulled himself free and started to fade into the crowd. "Do people a favor," he was saying, "and see what you get. I'm an honest man, I am. I fought three years with General Grant, I did. Nobody calls me a thief." Some people in the crowd hissed, and some laughed.

Mike realized there was no way he could get back the two dollars. He stood there helplessly as the crowd drifted away. The family was still babbling. The mother moved her bags closer together and put the children on top of them. The father was counting and recounting the money in his hand.

"Let me see," said Mike. He counted money in the man's open palm. There was a fifty-cent bill, a silver quarter, a three-cent bill, a five-cent postage stamp encased in brass, and a token from Lord and Taylor's Store worth one cent.

This was the money that was being used in March of 1867. The Civil War had come to an end only two years before. Silver and copper coins were rare because people were hoarding them. Times were so bad that people distrusted the new paper money coming out of the treasury.

"Eighty-four cents," said Mike. "You should have ninety-three cents. He stole nine cents from you. *Neun* cents. *Gonif.*" He walked away.

At the side of the square he turned and looked back. The family was still there, waiting. The father was still counting the money in his palm.

Mike walked back. "Where do you want to go?" he asked. The father shrugged. Two of the four children had finished their knishes and were crying. The grandmother was coughing in the dry cold.

"You want a place to stay?" Mike made a sign of sleeping.

The mother looked around wildly at the bustling street and the counting houses and warehouses. "*Ja, ja!*" she said.

"All right," said Mike. "I'll take you."

An hour later Mike was running up the stairs at Magnolia Court with a one-dollar bill in his hand. His sister Feena was running behind him.

"Where'd you get it?" she shouted. "Let me see it."

Mike knocked on Mrs. Thomas' door and then burst in. "Mrs. Thomas, I have a boarder for you," he said. "Mr. Moisha Cohen. Here's his money." Feena watched in puzzled silence as Mrs. Thomas wrote out the receipt for a week's rent and gave Mike a big iron key.

When they were back in the hall, Feena wailed, "Tell me! Tell me!" until Mike pulled her red pigtails and bounded down the stairs ahead of her. Feena clattered behind him. Her legs were even thinner than Mike's. She was one inch shorter than he was and one year younger—just turned thirteen.

Out in the street, the Cohens were waiting by a

wagon. Mike counted out money for the driver and gave Mr. Cohen the receipt and the key.

"Six-K," said Mike, tapping on the steel key tag. "Six-K. Six-K. That's your flat."

"Six-K," Mr. Cohen repeated.

"Take them up to Six-K, Feena," Mike commanded, and soon a straggly line of children and bags and boxes began to crawl up the six flights to the Cohens' new home. Then Mike took Mr. Cohen to the grocery store while Feena showed Mrs. Cohen how to arrange beds and baggage to make some room in their tiny quarters. Cracks in the windows had to be stuffed to keep the cold out. Water had to be brought up from the basement, seven floors below. And finally, the stove had to be coaxed alive.

It was dark when Feena and Mike finally stepped out into the smelly hallway and pushed the door closed. A shoulder stopped it short.

"Boy," said Mr. Cohen. He fumbled in his palm, counting to himself, and the next thing Mike knew, he was holding a silver quarter in his fist.

"Thanks!" Mike said, and he and Feena ran into the street and down to their own entrance.

Little Pat Brady was just going in, carrying a covered pail.

"Look what I have!" said Mike. "A quarter! My mother can make the best stew in New York for a quarter. That's what we'll have tonight for supper—lamb stew."

Pat put down the pail and turned the dull silver piece over again and again. "It's heavy. It's bigger than a shilling," he exclaimed. He flipped it into the air, and Mike caught it.

"Is that your supper in the pail?" asked Feena.

"No," said Pat as he picked it up again and started up the stairs. A wisp of strange smelling steam curled from under the lid.

Feena nudged Mike and whispered in his ear, "It's soup from the police station. Mrs. Brady doesn't have any money."

"Let me see what they give out at the police station," said Mike as they caught up to Pat on the landing. The little boy stuck out his tongue and slammed the door behind him.

"Michael Timothy!" Feena exclaimed. "Hold your tongue." Mike ran up the stairs three steps at a time and burst in the doorway to their flat.

His mother grabbed him and sat him down in

a chair. "Where have you two been?" she cried. "I was along the street a dozen times looking in the alleys for you and down those holes in the street. Even looking under the horses' hoofs! Where were you?" Even with Mike seated, his mother's head was only a few inches above his. She was a tiny woman with a knot of black hair on the back of her head and bright green eyes.

"We were helping a family move into 6-K." Mike held out the quarter in his dirty hand. His mother took it, wiped it on her apron, and put it in a small jar, the one for the rent money.

"That's more than your father made today," she said, stirring a pot on the stove.

"Come here," said a deep voice by the window. It was their father. Something was wrong. It was too early for him to be home from work.

His thick fingers curled around their shoulders as they sat on the cot beside him. The dying daylight brought out the wrinkles in his red neck and his freckled forehead.

The family across the alley was eating already. Nobody said anything until Mike's stomach started to speak for him.

"What are we having for supper?" he asked.

"Potato soup," said his mother.

"I thought we could have lamb stew," said Mike. His father put his hand on his shoulder. There was a long silence.

"You'd better get used to potatoes for a good while," said Mrs. Cullen. "Your father lost his job at the factory today."

CHAPTER TWO

Sheamus Cullen Makes His Mark

THAT night Mike woke up with a start. His mother and father were talking at the table a few feet away from his head. They stopped when they saw him move, and his mother pulled the blanket over his shoulders. He knew it was almost morning because he could hear Mr. Polachek on the other side of the partition getting dressed to go to the bakery. Mike closed his eyes, but he couldn't go back to sleep.

After a while his mother started whispering again. "Sleeping with other people in a hole no bigger than a cow stall! And no space outside either! No room even for the sun to shine down. Just walls everywhere. Why did we come here, Sheamus? Why didn't we stay in Ireland?"

"Because the land was against us," Mr. Cullen said.

"But my brother would have helped us for another year."

"The poor helping the poor."

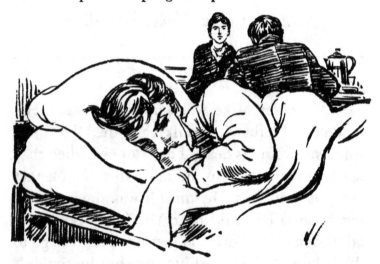

"At least, there we had friends. This year the crop would have been good. Who do you have here? A. S. Smith Sons? They gave you the door today. That Pearsal Furniture factory? They wanted you for a month, and then they didn't want you any more."

Mike's father sighed. "When they need men, they'll run through the streets looking for them,

Nora. And an hour after the job is done, they close the door on your back."

"But Finnegan has held a job now for four months."

"He's a skilled man."

"And O'Hara? He pushed a plow on the patch next to your father's these fifteen years. He has a job here in America."

"His cousin helped him, Nora. His cousin that works in the city office." Mr. Cullen sighed again. "Anyway, it's all luck. You know that. The day we moved into this place, my luck turned."

"Then let's move out. Let's go away where we can see the trees again and the soil God made to walk on. Even if we worked for a farmer like four animals and got a pot of stew and a crust of bread, it would be better than starving here."

"I need a job I can count on for from now to Christmas. I need a man to work for I can trust. That's what I need!" Sheamus Cullen hit his fist on the table.

"Shhh now, Sheamus! You'll wake up Michael again."

But Mike was awake. He was thinking of the sign he'd seen:

JOBS IN THE WEST
CALLAHAN CONSTRUCTION CO.
SEE MR. RYAN AT *THE GREEN*.

The Green opened at seven o'clock. The first customers in the coffee house were junior clerks on their way up to ice cold offices where they had to have stoves lighted and glowing by eight o'clock. A little before eight, senior clerks dropped in to the restaurant for coffee to warm their insides— "just in case the junior clerks didn't do their jobs." Between eight and nine you heard conversation about iron works and weaving mills, about secondhand rifles and firsthand biscuits—about any stock or bond that was being bought and sold by the brokers. About ten o'clock the brokers spilled out onto the sidewalks and started trading with each other and their customers. In the Green there was an hour of peace. It was this hour that Dr. Thomas Durant, managing director of the Union Pacific Railway, took to have his morning cup of coffee.

On this day he was tired and peeved. He had been up half the night trying to persuade some friends from Newport to put money in the Union Pacific Railway. They had turned him down. And this morning he had learned that the snow was still thick in Nebraska. Work on the section running westward into Wyoming could not begin for weeks yet. But in California, where the Central Pacific Company was building a railroad eastward from Sacramento, the weather was fine.

The Union Pacific and the Central Pacific were already fierce rivals.

Dr. Durant was hanging up his coat when Mr. Ryan rushed over to him and tipped his hat.

"Good morning, Dr. Durant," he greeted. "Fine cold weather, isn't it?"

"I'm not at your service now, Mr. Ryan," Dr. Durant said snappishly.

"But Major Callahan is very worried," said

Ryan, as fast as he could speak. "He's bought materials to build your railroad bridges. He's hired men. But he's afraid you're angry with him. He can't understand why you won't sign the contract you promised him."

Dr. Durant snorted. "You know very well why I'm angry. I found out Major Callahan bought secondhand wooden piles out of New York Harbor to use in Union Pacific Railway bridges. Tell him never to buy anything secondhand if he wants work from me. You may pick up his contract this afternoon in my office."

"Thank you, sir. I will," said Mr. Ryan. He bowed and turned away. Dr. Durant stooped over to flick some mud off his shoe when the door behind him opened, and Sheamus Cullen walked in with Mike.

"Good morning, sir," Mike's father said, tipping his hat. "Are you Mr. Ryan?"

"No, sir!" exclaimed Dr. Durant. He stalked back into the tavern where his coffee was waiting for him.

"Welcome. I'm Tom Ryan," said Ryan to Sheamus Cullen, in a friendly whisper. "Are you a man from County Sligo?"

"I'm from County Clare."

"What part?"

"Ardrahan in Carloe parish."

"I know it well. Lovely land. And you're look-ing for a job with Major Tim Callahan?"

"Yes, I am."

"You couldn't do better. Tim is the salt of the earth. Why, he'd give you the shirt off his back if you were working for him. Sit down at this table. And this is your son?"

"Michael. Yes. And I'm Sheamus Cullen."

"A fine young man; and Sheamus, he looks just like yourself."

Mike was surprised that Mr. Ryan didn't rec-ognize him from the day before. "Everyone says I look more like my mother," Mike said. But no one was listening to him.

"Mr. Ryan—" Mike's father began.

"Call me Tom," said Ryan. "And so you wish to join in the great work of America today which is to bring the West and the East together. Trade between them now must pass through the fierce waves of Cape Horn. Passengers must go by the uncomfortable stagecoach. What America needs is a link of steel rail between Omaha and the

West Coast—the Union Pacific Railroad." He took a sheaf of papers out of his pocket.

"And the wild Indians, Tom? Do they still live in the West?" Mr. Cullen inquired.

"A vanishing race. Do you know, you'll find bits of land out West that look just like County Sligo? A whole acre of land can be bought for almost nothing. Now. Here's the contract, Sheamus, that will take you to the West at no cost to yourself."

"Contract?" said Sheamus, looking at the long white paper with the tiny words printed on it. "In County Clare a man's word is worth a dozen contracts with his name marked in ink on them."

"Your word is good enough for me, Sheamus, but here in America everything must be done by contracts. Everything must be written out."

"What's that thing say?" Mike's father asked.

"It says you go to work for Tim Callahan, the best boss in the world, as soon as you get off the train."

"And how long will the job last, Tom? I had one job here in New York that lasted only from lunch to suppertime."

"I give you my word, Sheamus, it will last till the completion of the great Union Pacific Railroad. A pen and ink, please, waiter." Ryan glanced at his pocket watch.

"And how long will that be, please?" asked Mike's father.

"Oh, at least a couple of years if they don't have to drill any tunnels," said the waiter, putting a sharp pen and a pot of ink on the table.

Mike blushed as his father took the pen in his thick, calloused fingers and studied the paper. It was upside down. Mr. Ryan could see Sheamus Cullen didn't know how to read.

"I have to be running along in a minute, Sheamus," said Mr. Ryan in a loud voice, "to buy some brand new wooden piles for the bridges of the Union Pacific Railroad." He looked behind him to make sure Dr. Durant had heard him.

"And how much does the job pay, Tom?" Mike's father asked.

"A silver dollar for every day you work, and the best food you'll get in any railroad camp in the union. You leave tomorrow morning, and you'll be at work next week."

"Next week," Mr. Cullen repeated. "Next week. It must be a great ways to the West if I won't get there until next week." He fingered the contract. "Is it as far as from the top of Ireland to the bottom?"

"It is—three times as far, and then some to spare —but what do you care, seeing as Tim Callahan is paying your fare?"

Sheamus gave the pen to his son. "It's a big step, but I'm willing to take it. Put my name there at the bottom, Mike."

"What about me?" said Mike. "I want to go too." The men laughed. "I'm strong as an ox."

"And twice as stubborn," said his father. "Put my name there."

"What about Mother and Feena? Why can't we all go together?" Mike turned the paper right side up.

"Be quiet, Mike." Sheamus Cullen hit the top of the table with his fist. It always made him angry to have to show that he didn't know how to read or write.

Mike started to write the letters of his father's name. "I heard the West was three thousand miles away," he said under his breath.

"Oh, it's barely fourteen hundred," said the waiter. "It's not like crossing the sea."

Mike's father took the pen. "Fourteen hundred

miles!" he said. "And my wife and children here in New York! You better take them after all."

Ryan threw up his hands. "We're not in the transportation business," he said. "But sign your mark, Sheamus, and we'll see if there's some room in the car for your boy."

Mike threw down the pen and jumped across the room. "I won't take up any room," he cried. "I'm small as a squirrel." He sat in a chair, tucked his legs underneath him, and scrunched himself up into a ball. "Say I can go, Mr. Ryan!"

Ryan smiled broadly. "Small as a squirrel and strong as an ox. That's how they make them in County Clare, waiter. All right, Sheamus, sign your mark, and I'll take the boy."

Mike whooped. Dr. Durant looked up from his paper and scowled.

"I think the doctor is afraid wild Indians have descended on us here," whispered the waiter, as Sheamus Cullen clenched the pen and marked a broad "X" beside his name.

CHAPTER THREE

Rolling West

MRS. CULLEN refused to stay in New York. "What is that contract thing but a piece of paper?" she said. "What would you do if you got to the West and this Major Callahan man didn't need you at all?" Mr. Cullen argued and argued, but Mike's mother shook her head and said, "We must stay together."

And so the little green bag, which had never been opened, was opened now. A silver cup belonging to Great-grandfather Cullen and a gold chain that came from far back in Mrs. Cullen's family—these were put on the table with a gold ring. There was also a tiny sack of coins saved in case of a death in the family. Mrs. Cullen threw this onto the table too with a sigh. It reminded her of their little son Peter, who had died during the crossing and had been buried at sea. "If we had used this money to buy water for Peter in his fever," she said, "he might be sitting with us here today. We must stay together."

Sheamus Cullen spent the rest of the day trudging from jewelry store to jewelry store while Mike went to the train station. They both returned at dusk with bad news. A ticket to Omaha cost twenty-six dollars. The best price Mr. Cullen had been able to get for the gold and silver was twenty-three dollars.

"Then tell Ryan you can't go," said Mrs. Cullen. She and Feena stopped packing.

"But I signed the contract," Mr. Cullen protested.

"Tell him you can't go. Tell him I'm sick. Hurry now."

Mike and his father returned in an hour. "Mr. Ryan has given Dad his word he'll look after the two of you while we're gone!" Mike exclaimed.

"Yes, and the first pay I get, he'll send you out on the railroad," Mr. Cullen added, sitting down and warming his hands. "He's a fine man, Tom Ryan is."

"Tom Ryan!" Mrs. Cullen scoffed. "I never heard his name before today. Tell him I want no favors from him—unless he wants to make room for Feena and me on the train tomorrow."

"Nora, the train leaves in a few hours only!" cried Mr. Cullen. "Where would I find him at this time of night?"

"Find out at The Green where he lives, and go to his home. Go ahead, man."

Mike and his father returned to the cold, dark streets. Feena and her mother heard the hours

pass: ten o'clock struck, eleven, and twelve. They were dozing when Mike rushed up the stairs.

"It's settled!" he announced. "For twenty-five dollars, Mr. Ryan will arrange for you and Feena to go with us."

"Where does that money go, into his own pocket?" asked his mother. "That's some arrangement, that is! What will we have left to buy food with, I'd like to know?"

"Hush, Nora, and listen," said Sheamus Cullen, closing the door. "On top of that there's to be a

man in charge of all the other men on the train. And do you know who that is?" He looked from Feena to Nora in the dim light of the stove.

"Himself," Mike exploded.

"Sheamus Cullen himself," his father repeated. "And do you know how many men I have in my charge?"

"A thousand," said Feena.

Mike and his father laughed.

"How many?" asked Mrs. Cullen.

"Twenty-three."

"Twenty-three men!" she exclaimed. "The next thing you know, you'll be a foreman." And she got up from the chair and threw her arms around him.

A few hours later, Mike found himself standing on a freight platform in New Jersey, holding a list of the twenty-three names in his mittens.

"Mat Aroon," he whispered.

"Mat Aroon," his father shouted.

"Here," said a voice in the crowd gathered around them. The men's faces were like the pinched faces that had gathered on village greens at home. Their voices were the same meek voices of men who had failed, who were forced to go westward to look for luck.

"Phelan Byrne," whispered Mike.

"Phelan Byrne!" his father called out.

"He'll be here," someone said. "He's gone to mail a fat letter to his sweetheart in Killarney."

Sheamus Cullen paused. "Cheer up," he said. "It's few men can boast they have a free ride today to Omaha. Do you know what the gentry pay to ride the same rails? Seven cents a mile. Many a Yankee would lay down his hoe to be in your shoes, my boys."

"Thanks to Tim Callahan!" shouted Mr. Ryan from the door of a little shack marked, "Office." He turned to Mrs. Cullen, who was standing next to him, and said in a low voice, "You'll never know what a lot of trouble you put me to, Mrs. Cullen. But never mind that; I've finally arranged everything, so if you'll just pass me the . . ." He winked solemnly and slipped the twenty-five dollars into his pocket.

"Show us to our seats, if you please, Mr. Ryan," replied Mrs. Cullen. "Come along, Feena."

They passed a dozen boxcars and then Major Callahan's equipment—two flatcars stacked with wooden piles and a car loaded with iron braces and parts for a pile driver. "Just make yourselves comfortable," said Ryan, motioning into a small boxcar. It was loaded to the ceiling on one end with crates. On the other end were bolted a half dozen narrow benches.

"Twenty-five people in this space!" Mrs. Cullen exclaimed.

"Only till St. Joseph."

"And how far is that?"

"Only a few days." Ryan's broad smile disappeared from the doorway as the men swarmed in, looking for seats. In a moment there were none.

"I told you that's *my* seat!" shouted a lanky blond boy from Boston.

"Faith, it's mine," shouted an Irishman. "Cullen, how on earth can we all fit into this box?"

Sheamus Cullen turned to ask Ryan the same question, but Ryan had disappeared. As Mr. Cullen leaped into the corner where the two men were struggling, the squeal of car couplings was heard. The car jerked forward with a bang. They had started their trip to the Missouri River.

New Jersey, Pennsylvania, Ohio—the track cut through tidy farms and then through a wilderness of uncleared land, the first that Mike and Feena had ever seen. They sat at the tiny window, their noses glued to the cold pane, watching the enormous continent unfold.

"Who owns all that land?" Mike wanted to know. One Irishman said it belonged to rich men for hunting. The boy from Boston said it belonged to the government. They argued about this for two days.

In Indiana the train halted in a town where a new iron shop faced the tracks. A large sign was posted on it:

"MEN WANTED. TWO DOLLARS A DAY."

"What does that mean?" Mike asked. None of the Irishmen could believe that if a businessman wanted help, he would be willing to pay so much. They discussed the sign all day. Toward evening Sheamus Cullen noticed that there were only twenty-two men in the car. A middle-aged man from Vermont was missing. Sheamus guessed he had jumped train to take the two-dollar job.

In Chicago they sat in the freight yards all day. A dapper little man in a brown bowler stuck his head in the door and asked, "Any of you boys blacksmiths? Carpenters? I have a job for you."

"Get away, man," Sheamus Cullen thundered. "We're going to work for Major Tim Callahan on the Union Pacific."

"Any bakers?"

Mr. Cullen chased him away. Nevertheless, the next day the blond boy and a friend of his were missing.

After eight days in the boxcar they reached St. Joseph on the Missouri River. Mr. Cullen reported to the steamship office and was told that his men were to unload all of Callahan's equipment onto the dock and wait for the next lumber boat coming up from the Mississippi.

"Keep an eye open, and if you see anyone sneaking off . . ." Mr. Cullen muttered to his wife and Feena as he and Mike went to help. The men were making jokes about this unforeseen work.

"Too bad Ryan isn't here to help! . . . Yes, with his contracts to make us a bonfire! . . . Oh, I'm sure he'd want to unload the whole train by himself."

At midnight they were awakened by a whistle on the river. They worked by lamplight to load the steamboat so that the captain could cast off at dawn.

Sheamus Cullen counted and recounted his men. There were seventeen, now fourteen, then nineteen.

"Sit down and eat something," Mrs. Cullen insisted. She'd gotten soup from the steamboat's galley and had laid out some bread and cheese on a bench by the paddle-wheel box.

"The men are running off!" hissed Mr. Cullen.

"What can you do about it?" Mrs. Cullen demanded. "If they want to break their word to Callahan, all they have to do is open their wings and go. Bad luck to them. Let the police put them in prison."

"Do you think Major Callahan will want the likes of me if I bring him a half dozen men instead of twenty-three?"

"Sit down, Sheamus. It's not the Irish lads would betray you and break their word. It's the Yankees. There were four with us in New York, and now there's one left only. If you leave him in St. Joseph, there's an end to your worry."

The giant paddle began to shake and squeak in

its box. The boat churned away from the dock and headed north into a black mist. Mr. Cullen's soup got cold in the bowl in front of him.

"Feena," said Mrs. Cullen. "Make your father happy. Go see if there are nineteen Irish lads on the boat."

Feena walked forward. The paddle wheel slapped the water below with a steady rhythm. Steven Dooley was talking to a sailor.

"One," said Feena to herself.

She looked into the window of the smoking room and saw Frank Mulvaney dozing on a bench. "Two," she said.

In front of the smoking room, ties were stacked twenty feet high. Feena breathed in deeply. She could smell the Mississippi forest where the ties had been cut only a week or two before. She reached up to a tie that jutted out like a branch and grabbed it. A second later she had climbed to the top of the stack. There the ties lay flat, like an upper deck. She walked to where the stack came to a point in the bow of the boat. Directly below, Sean Burke was sitting in a coiled hawser, watching the first rays of the sun strike the trees on the western bank.

"Three," said Feena.

A middle-aged woman was sitting with Sean. She wore a gray shawl and a patched skirt, which she clasped around her knees with big work-worn hands. Her voice rose on the breeze to where Feena was standing. "Did you ever work for this Callahan before?"

"No," said Sean.

"You think you'll clear a dollar a day? Don't you know he can charge you fifty cents a day for food when you're out on the prairie, a thousand miles from the nearest store?"

"As long as I can put a few pennies in my pocket, I'm satisfied."

"They can't work after it freezes, you know. Come January, you'll be back on the siding in Omaha with no job and nothing in your pocket —if the Indians don't get you."

"Mr. Ryan said the Indians all went up into Canada."

"Canada!" the woman laughed. "If the British came and killed your cattle, would you run away?" Sean snorted.

"Well, Indians have lived on those plains for a thousand years." She pointed to the west bank.

"They're not going to run away to Canada just because you railroad boys come and ruin their pasture. They'll take every Irish scalp they can get their hands on. They're a proud people. They like to die fighting."

"I'm not frightened of them, wherever they are," replied Sean slowly.

"Maybe you're not. But I know one thing that does frighten you. Your contract." Sean grunted. "They told you they'd put you in prison if you broke the contract, didn't they?" He didn't answer. "Did they tell you how much a contract is worth in the West? It's worth this." She snapped her fingers.

"Come with me and my two sons. You won't regret it. I can teach you a trick or two, and you'll have a hundred and sixty acres this time next year. I'm not promising you wages or anything. All I say is, you work for me and you'll have a hundred and sixty acres of your own this time next year."

"Much obliged to you, but I have to get some sleep now." Sean got up and left.

Feena clambered down the side of the stack and jumped onto the deck squarely in front of the woman.

"What do you mean, trying to take Sean away?" she demanded. "If you do that again, my dad will throw you into the river!"

The woman looked up at Feena with wide, round eyes. "So you're the foreman's daughter! Do you want your mother to live in a coalbin next to the tracks all her life, or would you like to have a farm of your own? Tell your father that I'll take your whole family, all four of you. Go ahead. Tell him."

St. Joseph, White Cloud, Brownsville, Peru— the steamboat wound its way up the Missouri. At every landing, Sheamus Cullen watched his men to see who was walking down the gangplank. Between stops he watched the woman, who was called Widow Husker. He caught her once talking to Mat Aroon and Patch Daly, and once to the "Yankee," Johan Hartz. But by the time the box cottages and tall statehouse of Omaha came into view, he was sure all his Irish boys were loyal.

When the widow debarked with her two brawny sons, Mike and Feena helped them lead off a team of horses and their covered wagon. Meanwhile Major Callahan's equipment was being loaded onto flatcars at the dock. That night the Cullens slept in the Emigrant House. It was the first good sleep they'd had in ten days.

At 6:00 A.M., a bell announced the departure of the train to North Platte, the end of the rail line. The men piled sleepily out of their bunks to begin the last lap of the trip.

Sheamus Cullen got them all into a passenger car and then proudly counted noses in the dawn light. No matter how he counted, there were only seventeen men in the car.

Sean Burke, Mat Aroon, and Patch Daly were missing.

CHAPTER FOUR

Attack!

Oh! What's that?" exclaimed Mrs. Cullen.
Sean and Mat and Patch were gone, but their
places had been taken by a new passenger who sat
bolt upright in a seat all by himself, staring out at
the telegraph line that loped along beside them.
He wore a broad black hat with little crossed brass
muskets on the crown and the bright blue blouse
of the U. S. Cavalry. Below the waist he was
naked, except for a cloth wrapped between his
legs and two brass spurs strapped to his feet.

"It's an Indian," said Mike, guessing.

"What's he doing with that gun? Somebody get
him off the train before he kills all of us." The Indian turned and looked at Mrs. Cullen. He was

just a little older than Mike. His brown face was covered with a soft fuzz, and one leg was bandaged from ankle to knee.

"Me got sick leg," said the Indian without any expression at all. He turned around and looked out at the prairie again.

They had obviously reached the West. Herds of antelope flickered over the plains in the distance. An occasional adobe ranch sat in the middle of furrowed acres. The stations along this part of the line were only one year old. They stood alone, except for a few sod huts, where an occasional covered wagon waited for spring to make the push west into new farmland.

By late afternoon, Sheamus Cullen had convinced his wife that she wouldn't be scalped. "Didn't Ryan say that all the bad Indians were moving north into Canada?" he said.

This Indian didn't look any too good to Mrs. Cullen. She was nervous when Mike and Feena slipped into the seat next to him.

"What's your name?" asked Mike.

"Red Leaf," was the reply.

"Who's your chief?" Feena chimed in.

"My chief Andrew Johnson."

"That doesn't sound like an Indian name," said Feena.

"Of course not," said Mike. "Andrew Johnson is the President of the United States."

"Don't be afraid of him," said the conductor, stretching up to light the fat candle in the glass ball above their heads. "He works for the Army."

There was an ear-splitting crash. Mike and Feena were hurled onto the floor at Red Leaf's feet. Clouds of steam started pouring past the windows. A loud hissing sound was broken by whooping and shouting.

Mike was climbing to his feet when something slammed against the carriage. A cluster of splinters appeared on the wall. Someone was firing at them.

"Indians!" a man shouted.

"Get down, Mike." His father's heavy hand pulled him flat on the floor again.

"Kill him!" screamed a woman, pointing at Red Leaf, who was loading his gun with a look of wild hatred on his face. But instead of aiming at the woman, he poked his gun through the shattered glass and squinted through the steam at the attackers. "Shoot! Shoot!" he cried to the other passengers.

"Stay down, Mike," his father said again. "What do you know about Indians?"

Feena broke off the splinters and put her eye to the bullet hole. Through the steam she saw a pony's head coming straight for the train and behind it a torch held by a man crouching on the pony. Red Leaf's gun went off above her. The rider slid down with his torch, and the pony veered away.

Red Leaf grunted, "One dead," and loaded again.

The door at the end of the carriage was flung open, and a strange figure entered. He had a red and black face, and as he lurched forward, steam poured off his clothes.

"They're trying to burn us up—burn the whole train—throwing torches," he stammered. It was the fireman. He'd been scalded when the boiler burst in the locomotive.

"Where are we, anyway?" someone asked.

"Only five miles from Plum Creek," the fireman moaned. "But the wind's blowing—they'll never hear the shooting."

Red Leaf pulled in his gun and reloaded again. "You run to Plum Creek?" he asked the fireman.

"Then you? . . . you? . . . you?" He pointed at different men crouched around the fireman.

"I'll go!" said Mike, and immediately felt his father crush him against the floor again.

"Me no run," said Red Leaf. "Me got sick leg." He stuck his gun back out the window. There was a lull in the shooting.

"Are you fast?" the fireman asked Mike.

"Yes," said Mike, as his father said, "No, no."

"Well, he'd better get off to Plum Creek then— if you want to be alive—when morning comes."

"All right," Sheamus Cullen said. He knew Mike was fast.

Mike felt his father's hand relax. "Be careful!" his mother said. "Be careful, Michael!"

A dozen passengers crowded into the back of the carriage to see Mike out. Feena pressed a biscuit into his hand—as if he were going off to school.

"I'll be back in an hour," he whispered as the night wind hit him. "Which way is it?"

"That way," a voice answered. "You'll have to run around the whole train—"

Mike had slipped off the coupling and into the snow between two ties. He crawled quickly away from the locomotive, where the Indians seemed to

be gathered, and back under two cars to the caboose. So far no Indian had seen him—he hoped.

Mike took a deep breath and darted out onto the
prairie. The crusted snow broke under his feet. He
was sure he could be heard for miles. He ducked
behind a hillock, panting.

From here he could see the whole train—a long
black shape in the darkness. The locomotive was
tilted at a crazy angle, its fire still heating the empty
boiler. The iron plates were red hot, casting a
strange light over the snow. Mike could see a

crowd of Indians silhouetted against the light. Their tomahawks were ripping into the baggage wagon. Heavy crates were thudding into the snow.

Mike raced to another hillock. From here he could see even better. A cascade of bricks, bales, and boxes poured out of the baggage car. You could smell the coffee from ripped bags and oil from broken barrels. But the Indians weren't looking for food. They were rummaging through the wreck for ribbons to tie to their scalp locks and lace to put on the manes and tails of their ponies. Two

Indians were playing with bolts of velvet, racing each other around the locomotive as the cloth unrolled in the snow.

The cab of the locomotive was burning now. An Indian took a burning plank and climbed onto the roof of the baggage car with it. He was trying to set the train on fire.

Mike wanted to see more. He ran ahead again, passed the locomotive and then cut back to the track. From here it was easy to see how the Indians had stopped the train. They had pried up the tracks and piled ties beneath them. When the locomotive hit the rails, the boiler burst.

A flame shot out of the baggage car, lighting up the track right up to where Mike was crouching. He decided it was time to run. Just then, he saw one of the shadows moving away from the train toward him.

He stepped off along the track as fast as he could. The ties were like black stripes against the snow. Hopping from one to the next, he stepped out too far, slipped between the ties, and got a handful of splinters. As he got up, he looked back and saw the same shadow moving against the snow.

This time he found his stride. Plum Creek was

five miles away. He stepped out faster. His feet hit the ties—*pock, pock, pock!* He could hear the feet of someone behind him hitting in almost the same rhythm. His neck began to sweat, and his back felt bare and very broad.

Now the other feet couldn't be heard any more. Had the Indian given up the chase? Mike didn't dare look around, but he slowed for a second. Suddenly the feet could be heard again. Mike realized the Indian was gaining on him yard by yard. The icy night air sent a pain down into his chest, but he just breathed deeper and ran faster. Now the feet were hitting together again: *pock, pock, pock!*

Mike tried to get his knife out of his pocket. His legs were beginning to feel like wood. He could hear the Indian gaining on him again, and now there was another sound—a clicking coming from ahead of him. He peered into the darkness and made out a tiny light glowing on the tracks. The Indian behind him let out a whoop that turned Mike's blood cold and gave him another burst of speed.

Then the scream of a brake reached him, and before he knew it, he was piled up against a little car with two men on it. They were railroad men.

"Go back," he stammered. One of the men pulled him onto the car as a dark figure ran past and swerved off into the snow.

The other man shoved a pistol into Mike's hand. "Cover us," he said, and threw his weight onto the handle that propelled the car. Mike looked out into the night, with sweat pouring off

his face. Everything seemed to take the shadowy shape of an Indian.

The wheels of the car were turning slowly backward. The men strained and puffed. Mike looked down the track behind them. He saw three more shadows there. He stiffened his arm and pulled the trigger. By the light of the flash he saw there was nothing on the track at all. At the same instant the pistol bucked. The butt hit Mike in the chest and knocked him back.

The car picked up speed. The two men rocked back and forth on the handle, and soon they were rolling quickly through gusts of snow. Mike told his story as they approached Plum Creek.

"We'll get the troops out," said one of the men.

"Don't worry," said the other, puffing over the handle. They were telegraph linesmen who had come out on this handcar to fix a break in the line.

At Plum Creek there was one small square of light—the station house. They rushed in and found a tall, gaunt man asleep in a wicker chair beside a desk. One hand lay on a gold watch chain and the other on a telegraph key.

"Gandy!" shouted one of the linesmen as the

other one shook him by the shoulder. "Gandy, you know who made that break in the line? Indians. There's been a raid."

The man's eyes opened and his hand came to life on the telegraph key. He made a couple of clicks. "A raid?"

"They almost caught us. . . . Derailed a train too. . . ." The two men were talking at the same time. "This boy got away. . . . Send a message to Fort Kearny. . . . We've got to get the troops out, Gandy!"

"There's nobody at Kearny," the operator said slowly. "All the soldiers have been sent west." His hand moved again on the key.

"How about Willow Island? . . . Brady?"

"You'd be lucky if you could raise ten guns in the whole county." Mike's heart sank. "Wake up, North Platte," mumbled the operator, clicking the key again.

"North Platte!" said the linesmen. "That's better than a hundred miles from here."

"Well, that's the closest you can find troops," said the operator. "Wake up, North Platte!" And abruptly the telegraph began to click back.

"Tell them to hurry," Mike said, feeling very

useless. The life of his family depended on those clicking signals going over the wires to North Platte now. He sat down in a rocking chair next to the stove and picked splinters out of his hand. A big clock ticked on the wall. It said 9:13.

The telegraph key stopped. The operator turned in his chair and looked squarely at Mike. "You're in luck, boy. General Dodge is in North Platte tonight."

Mike jumped up. "Is he coming? I have to go tell my folks on the train."

"Sit down now and take a rest. I won't know for a few minutes." The operator started to clean his rifle, and the two linesmen went out to warn the farmers that Indians were nearby.

The room was silent except for the pendulum of the clock. Waves of red glow passed over the belly of the stove. Mike's head grew heavy. He focused hard on the clock. 9:21. Eight minutes had passed. He tried to imagine what might have happened in eight minutes back at the train. But his eyes wouldn't stay open. . . .

When Mike awoke, he was looking into the sooty face of a man who wore an enormous mustache. "Are you the boy who was on the train?" Mike nodded. "Come along quick now."

Mike looked at the clock. It said 5:39! He followed the man out the door through a group of glum farmers and into the cab of a locomotive. The engineer pulled a lever, and the giant wheels began to turn in a hiss of steam.

"How many Indians did you see, boy?" asked the man with the mustache. He was chewing on a piece of bread.

"About a hundred."

"And how many ponies?"

"Dozens."

"What were the Indians wearing?"

Mike thought hard. "Feathers on their heads. And robes. Striped robes."

"Sounds like Sioux Indians. We're in for a fight." The train was rolling quickly now. They passed a farmer's wagon moving toward the safety of Plum Creek. "Do you want to fight too, boy?" the man asked.

Mike rubbed his eyes. "Sure," he said.

"Well, there's your breakfast." The man laughed and handed him a piece of bread. "Now you're a soldier. Go back to the baggage car and get a rifle from Major North. Tell him I think the Indians are Sioux."

"Who should I say you are, sir?" asked Mike. He still didn't know whom he was talking to.

"General Dodge," the man said, putting his hand on Mike's shoulder. "I want to hear about your race with the Indian some time."

Mike ran back through the coal car and over the coupling between cars. He remembered that only a few hours ago he'd been running for his life across the same ground. Now he was safe with General Dodge, Chief Engineer of the Union Pacific Railway.

He opened the door to the baggage car and stepped into the darkness. A tall man was standing there.

"Major North?" Mike asked.

The man turned slowly. He had a broad, flat face, a hooked nose, and a long, stiff clump of hair. It was an Indian. Mike froze. The Indian looked down at him without moving.

Mike took a step away and bumped into another Indian seated on the floor, holding a rifle. The floor was covered with Indians, and they were all looking at him.

"Hello," said a voice.

"Hello," said Mike.

"I'm Major North." A short man in uniform approached Mike.

Mike noticed the Indians were wearing the same comical uniforms as Red Leaf. He relaxed and gave his message. Major North said a few gutteral words to the Indians. They jumped to their feet and started shouting. Mike ducked.

"Don't be afraid," said the major. "They're friendly Indians. They're Pawnees."

"Why are they shouting?" asked Mike.

"I told them they'd be fighting Sioux. They're happy because the Sioux are their old enemies." He laughed and shouted a word to the Indians. They quieted down. The train was coming to a halt.

Major North gave Mike a rifle, and together they slipped down onto the snow. The Indians ran forward silently to the top of a grade. Below was a strange sight. The Sioux had lighted a fire in front of the locomotive and were staggering around it. Some were wearing ladies' bonnets, and others were completely covered with calico and velvet. They fell in the snow and then got up again to dance some more.

"Looks like they got into a keg of whiskey," Major North whispered to General Dodge. "We're in luck." He gave a command in the Pawnee language, and the Indians flew down the side of the hill, whooping and hollering.

As they approached the train, Mike saw that the carriages were all gone! The only thing that remained between the locomotive and the caboose were some charred timbers.

A scream burst from the ground near Mike. He looked down and saw a young Sioux lying in the snow. A Pawnee was drawing his knife around the Indian's scalp. Mike looked on in horror. He thought of his mother and father and Feena. Had the same thing happened to them?

"Look," said General Dodge. "There's somebody!" Mike looked up at the blackened caboose and saw half a dozen men jump out, shooting at the retreating Sioux. Red Leaf was leading in spite of his limp.

Then Mike's father caught him in his arms. "Mike, Mike, thank heaven you're all right. And Feena kept telling us the whole night long not to worry."

They walked hand in hand to the caboose. A pearl-colored glow began to spread through the sky. The voices of the Indians faded over the hill behind them. Inside the caboose Mike could hear Feena's voice singing, "Michael Timothy! Michael Timothy!"

CHAPTER FIVE

Boom Town

IN THE fight at Plum Creek four men were killed—the engineer, a Mormon farmer on his way to Salt Lake City, Steven Burke, and Pat Casey.

Everything the Cullens owned had been burned. They rolled into North Platte late in the afternoon with only the clothes on their backs. But Mike and Feena felt more important than they had in their whole lives. They felt like heroes returning from the wars.

On one side of the tracks stood two long buildings marked: CASEMENT BROTHERS WAREHOUSE, surrounded by piles of coal and lumber. On the other side were two hundred shacks, tents, and makeshift buildings. The biggest of them was a patched brown tent from which snatches of singing could be heard. This was the Big Tent, where anyone with ten cents could try his luck at the games. The men who had lost their last ten cents stood outside watching a dog fight. Others roamed through the muddy streets, testing the sun by rolling up the sleeves of their checked shirts.

When Mrs. Cullen got off the train, a shout went up: "A woman in North Platte! Look, a woman!"

Around the station house there was complete confusion. Boys from rival stage companies competed for passengers traveling west. Freight outfits competed for their luggage. Brawny bull whackers rolled bundles and barrels down the platform to where an acre of horses, mules, carts, and wagons stood waiting. Mr. Cullen pressed through into the station house and asked a railroad employee where Major Callahan could be found.

"He's out at the end of the track with General Casement. Won't be back till tomorrow."

"I have fifteen men come from New York to work for him. Where can they sleep?"

The man shrugged. "Sleep on the benches." He motioned to the rough boards running around the waiting room.

The Irishmen stood back against the wall watching the hustle and bustle, very much as they had the day they arrived in America. Behind them a yellow poster was tacked to the wall. It said "GAMBLERS AND CONFIDENCE MEN NOT WANTED IN NORTH PLATTE."

There was a shot outside, and Feena began to cry. A small, burly man with tiny sunken eyes and bushy black eyebrows came up to her. He took off a dented bowler hat and said, "Don't be frightened, miss. Nobody in North Platte would dare to shoot at a lady. Was you by any chance on the train wrecked by the Indians?"

"That's right," said Mike.

The man took Mike's father by the arm. "You would please me elegant if you would stay in my shabeen. Whiteleather is my name." And before Sheamus Cullen could say even what his name was, Mr. Whiteleather was steering them past the dog fight in front of the big tent to a shack on which was written: *Rolling Belinda*.

Rolling Belinda was part house, part cart. Its walls were borrowed from broken boxcars, tacked together with rusty nails and painted with mud. It had a ridge pole spliced out of bits of timber and a roof of canvas, lined now with a foot of snow. Its floor was supposed to be dirt, but now it was inlaid with broken glass, splinters, and pebbles, all ground smooth by the boots of the men who had come to buy food through the winter.

Mr. Whiteleather led them past shelves of merchandise into a back shed. In the shed there lay two dirty mattresses and a pile of mud-stained

blankets and tarpaulins. "Here is a bed for the children and here, one for you, Mrs. Cullen. There's nothing to fear in *Rolling Belinda,* except maybe a little rough language, when the stove goes out."

Mr. Cullen laughed.

"You have a beautiful family," said White-leather, slapping him on the shoulder. Within a half hour Mike was peeling potatoes, Mrs. Cullen was cooking Mr. Whiteleather a stew, and Feena was darning Mr. Whiteleather's socks. Mr. Whiteleather was selling tobacco and provisions as fast as he could to men who came to hear about the Indian attack.

". . . There I sat blinded by that white steam hissing like a teakettle, and in the distance the Indians whooping and moaning—" Mr. Cullen said.

"What did that sound like?" asked a tall man.

"Wa wa wa oo wa wa oo!" said Mike from the corner, slicing potatoes into a rusty pot.

The men turned to look at him, some straight-faced and some doubled over with laughter.

"And what was the fair colleen doing?" asked the tall man. But Mrs. Cullen wouldn't say a word. Then five or six newcomers would push through the door, and Sheamus Cullen would have to start his story all over again. The men shouted and shoved until Mr. Cullen had to lead his wife and daughter away from the stove and back into the shed.

As he did so, Whiteleather's voice could be heard shouting, "Mind your manners there. The ladies are our guests. Watch your language, you hooligans. Why don't you put your pennies in this hat for the poor lady who lost all her belongings to the wild Sioux?"

With that, Whiteleather's dented bowler started circling the room upside down, catching copper and silver pieces for the Cullens. When Sheamus saw the bowler plop on the bar and the coins spill out, he nearly cried. "God bless you, every one of you. God bless you, Mr. Whiteleather. This is the finest thing as has happened to me since I came to your country seven long months ago. And now I must let my two girls get some sleep."

"More! More!" sang the men.

"Mike will stay for a minute," said Whiteleather as he rolled a barrel into the crowd. "Stand on that, Mike."

Mike stepped onto the barrelhead, rose up over the grinning faces, and found himself saying, "Well, it was like this: The Indians were throwing torches, you see, trying to burn us to Kingdom Come. And we were shooting back, shooting the ponies out from under them, like that. And there was this one Pawnee boy named Red Leaf. . . ."

Late that night Mike woke up as somebody ripped the blanket off him. He rolled into a ball, half expecting to hear a Sioux whoop.

"I'm freezing," said a small voice. It was Feena.

Mike sat up. His throat was dry and hoarse. How many times had he told the story of the Indian raid—six? seven?

"I'm freezing too," he said, groping for the covers. He spread another blanket over his sister, rolled under a tarp, pulled his collar up, and closed his eyes. In the perfect stillness a sad voice could be heard faintly from the next room.

"It's four years now since I've seen her, the most beautiful girl in all Killarney. Oh, there's many wanted to marry her, but she told them all, 'I'll wait for Phelan. Soon Phelan will bring me to America.' "

"It's Phelan," Feena whispered to Mike. "He's sad tonight."

"Tell me about her." That was Whiteleather's voice.

Phelan went on after a pause. "I can bring her over, but what'll she find when she gets here? Snow and mud. No, I have to have a house for her. That's what she would be getting in Ireland—a snug home for the children to come into."

"Do you have money to buy lumber and nails?"

"I do."

"Then I can get you land, cheap. Don't worry about that. How much can you spend for a beautiful piece of land, say a hundred and sixty acres? The nicest piece of land a man could dream of?"

"Well, I don't know."

Feena put her ear close to the wall. She could hear the sound of the table being cleared.

"That's what I have for her passage," Phelan went on. "That's for her passage. And that's for the wedding. And that's for a pair of fine horses and a plow. It took me ten years almost to save this money. . . ."

There was a thud and then silence, except for the prairie wind rattling the slats of the shack. Then a chair tipped over, and footsteps could be heard going slowly and heavily to the door. A few minutes later the door slammed shut and there was silence again except for the sound of deep breathing.

*A short, black-bearded man was standing
on a wagon*

"What happened, Mike?" whispered Feena. "What happened?" But Mike didn't answer. He was fast asleep again.

The next morning Mike woke up to the sound of cheering in the street. His mother and father and Feena had gone out. The cheering died down and a thin, strong voice, sharp as a whip crack, replaced it. Mike struggled into his shoes and ran through the store and out onto the street.

Mr. Whiteleather was standing under his sign, *Rolling Belinda,* picking his black fingernails with a little penknife. He smiled at Mike.

"Good news today," he said. "Track laying starts tomorrow morning." The crowd was cheering again.

Mike tied up his shoes before stepping into the mud. He could see his family at the back of the crowd listening to a short, black-bearded man who was standing on a wagon. The man slapped the sides of his leather coat as he waited for attention, knocking two revolvers together on a wide belt.

"Who's that?" asked Mike.

"Jack Casement. General Jack," said Whiteleather. "He lays all the track for the U.P. He's a fine speaker. Listen."

"The Central Pacific has got over the Sierra Madre Mountains. They claim they'll lay two hundred miles of track this summer. And do you know how they plan to do it? With Chinese. With five thousand Chinese right off the boat from Shanghai." The crowd roared.

"Are you going to let them beat us to Salt Lake City?"

"No!" answered the crowd.

"General Dodge says the track has to reach Fort Saunders by the first of November. That's three hundred miles. Those Eastern newspapermen say he's crazy. They say you can't do it. What do you say, boys?"

The crowd made a lot of noise again.

"Those New York reporters saw an Indian or two last summer. They think a few Indians can hold up the U.P. They can think again—those New Yorkers."

The men laughed. Mike walked to the edge of the crowd and stood next to Feena.

"There's only one thing can hold us up," said General Casement. He took off his fur cap and twisted it in his hand. Then he hit it against his knee and put it on again. "Just one thing," he repeated, scowling at the owners of the Big Tent and the other gambling casinos, who stood in their doorways scowling back.

"Last night another U.P. man was murdered."

"He was trying to shoot Charlie Cotter!" one of the gamblers yelled.

"Last night another U.P. man was murdered," Casement repeated. "That makes eighteen since the first camp was set up at Fremont. Eighteen men."

"Stick up for yourself, Charlie," another gambler called out.

"General Dodge has selected the next camp." There was a sudden hush across the crowd. "Julesberg." A ripple of excitement swept through the crowd.

"If there's any shooting in Julesberg, General Dodge will declare martial law," Casement announced. The gamblers jeered softly.

"Don't come to Julesberg!" shouted Casement. "Stay here." The gamblers started to whistle, "Put Two Bits on Number Twelve." And at the same time someone started singing, "The Rose of Killarney." It was Phelan. He staggered through the crowd and went up to General Casement.

"Excuse me, sir," he said. "Did you see it?"

"What?" asked Casement.

"I don't know," replied Phelan vacantly.

"What's the matter with you, man?" asked Casement, and he took off Phelan's hat. Underneath it was a huge mat of bloody hair.

"A man hit me, sir," said Phelan.

"What for?" asked Casement.

"I don't remember. I think it was for my money."

"Here's a man who's had the wits beaten out of him. Who did it?" shouted Casement.

Feena pulled her father by the sleeve. "I told you Mr. Whiteleather did something to Phelan," she said.

"Don't be silly," Sheamus Cullen retorted. "Mr. Whiteleather has been the soul of kindness."

"I heard him hit Phelan and carry him out into the snow," Feena protested.

"Be still now," said her mother.

"Who did it?" Casement demanded of Phelan.

Mike looked around. Mr. Whiteleather was moving back into the shadow of *Rolling Belinda,* his knife clenched in his fist.

"Who did it, man?" Casement asked once more, softly now.

"I don't remember," said Phelan. "Do you?"

Whiteleather stepped back out into the sunlight, closed his little knife, and smiled.

CHAPTER SIX

End of Track

GENERAL JACK CASEMENT'S office was a boxcar. It stood at the end of a strange procession called the boarding train. First there were several long cars for sleeping and eating, then some short ones for cookhouse, bakery, butcher shop, and general store. The office car was papered with maps and survey charts of Nebraska. A lanky man with a lean, haggard face and a ragged red mustache sat at the stove, cracking his knuckles. This was Major Tim Callahan.

"It's not my fault. It's the Indians!" he shouted. And then in a softer voice, "You have to help me out, Jack."

"You lost *everything* in the Plum Creek wreck?"

asked Casement. "Didn't you wire Omaha for re-placements?"

"What can I do, Jack? I don't have the cash to buy all that equipment again. Lend me a couple hundred piles and a hundred twelve-by-twelve's from your warehouse. I'll pay you back as soon as the Union Pacific pays me."

There was a knock at the door. Casement hitched up his mud-caked trousers and walked around the stove. "All right," he decided. "I'll do that for an old friend. I'll do it because this is your first contract with Dodge. Make a list of what you need, and don't worry so much. Things were a lot worse at the Battle of Gettysburg, weren't they?"

The two men laughed in a friendly way, warmed by the memory of the Civil War, which had ended only two years before. There was a second knock.

Callahan jumped out of his seat and opened the door. Below in the snow stood Sheamus Cullen in front of a straggly band of men. "Can you tell me where is Major Callahan?" Mr. Cullen asked.

"You're looking at him," Callahan said. "Are you from Ryan? Let's see your list." Sheamus handed up a rumpled piece of paper.

"Aroon, Mat Aroon!" Callahan called out.

There was no answer. The men looked blank and stamped their feet in the snow.

"You didn't tell me," Casement snorted, "that you were waiting for a trainload of greenhorns out of New York Harbor."

"Burke, Steven Burke!" Callahan went on. Again no answer.

Sheamus said, "The Indians put a bullet through his head at Plum Creek, sir."

"Indians again!" Callahan exploded, "cutting down my work crew." He turned to Casement. "We must have more troops guarding the railroad." He turned back to Sheamus.

"How about Byrne, Phelan Byrne? I suppose he was killed by the Indians too."

"No, sir, he was brained here in North Platte, only last night." Sheamus pointed to Phelan, who was sitting on a broken cask, knocking his feet together.

"If it isn't the Indians, it's the gamblers!" Callahan exploded again. "What can we do, Jack, to stop the gamblers from ruining the railroad?"

"What happened to that first man, Aroon?" demanded Casement.

"He broke his contract, sir. Sneaked off with a

farmer back in Omaha," Sheamus admitted sheepishly.

"You call yourself a foreman?" Callahan roared. "There are twenty-three men on this list. How many are you bringing me?"

"Fourteen," murmured Sheamus. "And my son. If you'll have him. He's a big boy. Strong—"

"A kid," Casement grunted, looking at Mike. "You don't need kids, Tim. You need men. And you need men who know bridge building—not farmers." He walked back into his office, disgusted. "If you can build the bridge over Lodgepole Creek with that crew, you're the best engineer in the U. S. A!"

Next morning at half past five, the mess tables in the boarding train were loaded with platters of meat, vegetables, and pie. At the same time General Jack Casement strode down the frost-glazed streets of North Platte with a long silver whistle around his neck. He climbed into his office and blew the whistle twice. A locomotive hooted and with a single lunge shook every man awake throughout the train.

At the Big Tent a handful of men spilled into the street and ran after the train. Some of them managed to catch the last car and swing up onto the roof, where they perched like a row of chicka-dees.

Now two more locomotives, coupled together, backed across the muddy siding to the rear of what looked like a long wood pile. Short white breaths punched up into the frosty sky, and the wood pile began to move along the track. This was the con-

struction train—fifty flatcars stacked with ties, rails, spikes, and provisions. Every morning these fifty cars would travel to the "front" and return empty in the afternoon.

Eight miles away, a dozen teams of horses and oxen were waiting at "end of track." Here the two trains came to a halt. Three hundred men piled out and stacked their rifles in the snow.

Everyone had his job except Mike, who watched.

The wood pile began to disappear as three carts started carrying ties out along a line of stakes. The stakes marked the grade that had been prepared

last fall. A man in each cart kicked the ties off the tail gate. A swarm of men dragged them onto the grade. From a distance the ties looked like a row of matchsticks marching toward California.

"We're laying a mile and a half today. So smooth that grade!" Casement was everywhere, his gloved hands planted on his hips, shooting out orders and encouragement.

"Where's Paskie? Didn't anyone wake him up? Where's the best tie slinger west of the Mississippi?"

"Got in a fight last night at the Big Tent," a man mumbled. "Broke two fingers."

Casement's face turned purple. His voice snapped out, "Start your rails!"

A dozen men jumped beside the rail cart, which sat in front of the boarding train, loaded with 28-foot iron rails.

"Hold!" Six men grabbed a rail on one side, six on the other. "Up, forward!" One gang yanked the rail to their shoulders and stepped forward. "Ready, down!" The rail plunged.

There was a clank as the back end of the new rail touched the last rail laid the year before. There was a thud as the front end fell along the wooden ties, pointed straight west.

"Hold! . . . Up, forward! . . . Ready, down!" And a second rail now lay parallel to the first.

"Hold! . . ."

Already the rail cart was moving over the loose rails. Behind it dozens of men closed in, spiked each rail to its ties, bolted the ends to its partners and tamped the ground beneath it where the sun was struggling to melt the frozen grade into mud.

The Union Pacific was growing west again.

"Major Callahan!" Casement called. "What's holding you up now? We'll have the track out to Lodgepole Creek before you get your first pile driven."

"Faster, Cullen!" shouted Major Callahan, as Mike and his father struggled to move the last of 250 piles from the train to a waiting wagon.

"I thought I told him to stay home," said Casement, pointing to Mike.

"You greenhorn, Cullen!" Callahan suddenly took Mike's place. "Grab the pile like this, man. There's no time to dawdle."

The first of Callahan's wagons groaned and creaked as it rolled out along the stakes toward Lodgepole Creek. A dozen men crawled over its tarp, looking for soft hollows where they could roost during the rough one-hundred-mile ride.

"Good-by, Michael," said Sheamus Cullen, hugging his son. "God keep you safe. Take care of your mother and sister now. I'll be gone six or seven months." He was panting for breath after the tussle with the piles. "Next year you can work on the railroad, too."

"I'm coming with you," said Mike stubbornly. He looked over his shoulder to see if Casement was watching.

"Get on board, Cullen!" shouted Callahan. A whip cracked. Six pairs of horses strained forward in harness. On the tall lead wagon, the driver flung the brake free and the wheels began to move. Couplings squealed and a smaller wagon swung into the tracks of the bigger one. Behind it a third wagon, even smaller, shivered and began to roll.

"No, Mike, stay down." Sheamus pushed Mike back into the mud. "No, Mike, don't follow. Next year. Next year."

The fourteen Irishmen clambered onto the lurching wagon train. They were headed west again.

Mike kicked at a frozen clod. Nobody wanted him. Could he return to North Platte? No, he must stick with "end of track" even if he had to sleep with the horses.

There was an idea, he thought. He would ask

General Jack to let him groom the horses. What harm could there be in that?

He turned and ran after Casement.

"Half the day gone and not a thousand feet laid," the general was complaining to a foreman. "Don't they know they're working for Jack Casement again? They're not being paid to take it easy and get fat."

Casement glowered across the prairie. He set his whistle between his teeth, blew twice, and climbed into his office.

Mike found the door shut in his face as the locomotive hooted and rolled onto new track. The ten cars of the boarding train passed by, one by one. The construction train followed—all fifty flatcars, half of them already empty. Finally the caboose passed, and Mike was left standing alone, staring east across the eight desolate miles to North Platte. It was very clear he wasn't wanted. Should he give up and walk home?

A voice questioned him from above. "Where's General Jack?" He looked up and saw the telegraph operator sitting on a pole. He was cutting down a wire that had been spliced to the telegraph line when the train moved up.

Mike was left standing alone

"He's in his office," Mike said.

"Run this telegram up to him," said the operator, shinning down the pole. He placed a folded piece of yellow paper in Mike's hand and then started winding up his wire. "Quick now."

Mike trudged back along the cars. Gray clouds were passing above, and a miserably icy rain began to sweep down the tracks. By the time he reached the first locomotive, "end of track" was far ahead again. It seemed to be advancing almost as fast as he could walk.

Mike caught sight of Casement's black fur hat moving among the workmen. He walked up to him and held out the telegram, waiting for the moment to ask him about the horses.

"Didn't the construction train take you home yet?" Casement snapped. With his thick gloves on, he was having trouble unfolding the telegram. "Everything slow today!" The rain whipped across the paper, splotching the words as he read them.

His eyes lighted as he made out the message, and for the first time Mike saw him laugh. He crumpled the paper into a ball, threw it into the wind, and blew his whistle.

The men stopped working and looked around, puzzled. It was too early in the day to quit.

"Gather round!" the foreman called out. They laid down their tools and started drifting closer to him.

Casement and the foreman stood shoulder to shoulder, making a list on the back of a slat.

"And the one with the scar on his cheek and the lanky walk," Mike heard Casement saying.

"That's Tennessee Markham," said the foreman, writing it down.

Casement caught Mike's eye. "What's your name, boy?" he asked.

"Mike," said Mike, ready to ask his question.

"Who hit your friend Phelan on the head?"

"It was Mr. Whiteleather," answered Mike.

"Whiteleather!" exclaimed the foreman. "He owns *Rolling Belinda*. Did you see him do it?"

"My sister and I were right there. We heard him."

"Put him down," said Casement. "If he sells whiskey, he can make trouble. What's he look like?"

"Short and stocky," said Mike, "with bushy eyebrows and a wart. On the left side of his nose.

Here." The foreman marked all this down. "General Casement, how would it be if I—"

But Casement wasn't listening. He was stepping up onto a cask of spikes. "We're quitting," he bawled at the men. "You boys have got too fat to work. Are you the same boys that laid two miles and four hundred feet last October 22nd? I can't believe it. About all you're good for now is to get in each other's way. Who taught you how to do that? The boys at the Big Tent? I bet you wish you were back there right now. Well, suppose I was to take you all back myself until the weather clears up."

The men looked at each other, not knowing whether to cheer or protest.

"I'm giving a party tonight for every man here who fought with the Confederacy or the Union. Don't come if you never carried a gun. And if you did carry one, bring it tonight. Hear me? The construction train leaves in a half hour. Everyone who fought in the Army meet me there." Casement walked away, grinning to himself. Mike stood in the way, his mouth open again.

"You want to stay with us," said Casement, taking the words out of Mike's mouth. "Tell the cook he should put you to work." And he strode off along the track.

Mike stood amazed. He was staying, after all! The track layers passed him, joking with each other and singing bits of marching songs. The empty tie wagons passed. Around the spoke of one wheel Mike saw a soggy piece of yellow paper. It was the telegram.

He slipped it off and opened it. The words were running together, but in the dark afternoon light the message was still clear:

DOCTOR DURANT HAS INVITED PARTY OF INVESTORS TO VISIT UNION PACIFIC. MAKE SURE ALL STATIONS CLEANED UP, ESPECIALLY AROUND END OF TRACK. GET RID OF ALL GAMBLERS, CONFIDENCE MEN, AND SUSPECTED CRIMINALS. USE WHATEVER MEANS NECESSARY. ACT SOON. SIGNED GRENVILLE DODGE

CHAPTER SEVEN

The Excursion

FEENA and her mother were sitting looking into the empty pot on the table.

"Very good stew, Mrs. Cullen," said Mr. Whiteleather, wiping his mouth with the back of his hand. "You're a fine cook. But I'm afraid we'll be parting company next week. I'm off for Julesberg with *Rolling Belinda*. Oh, Julesberg will be even wilder than North Platte, the way it looks."

A sharp command could be heard in the street, followed by angry voices. Feena went to the window and peered out. "Nothing but ruffians and thieves in these boom towns. The pack of them should be drowned in the River Platte." Mr. Whiteleather broke a splinter off the underside of the table and started picking his teeth.

"Where can we stay then," asked Mrs. Cullen, "if all the shabeens are going to Julesberg?"

"Best for you to go back to Omaha, respectable ladies like you," Mr. Whiteleather advised.

"They've just arrested a man," Feena exclaimed, "and they're marching him out of the Big Tent."

"Praise be the day!" said Whiteleather. "Who's doing the arresting?" He nudged Feena aside and looked out of the window himself. "Casement's men! Blood and tarnation!"

The voices swelled until they were right outside. Then the door was slapped open, and two wiry railroadmen entered. One was dressed mostly in the blue of the Union Army, the other in pieces of a Confederate uniform. "Who's Whiteleather?" said the man in blue.

"He's out in back. I'll go get him," said Whiteleather, retreating into the shed.

"Short and heavy, big eyebrows and a wart on the left side of his nose," the second man read on a scrap of paper. "Sounds more like *this* man."

"It was this one!" echoed the man in blue. And they ran after Whiteleather out the back door onto the prairie.

Feena and her mother watched, astonished. In the street two hundred armed men stood in two long lines sandwiching a dozen gamblers. Whiteleather was led protesting to the end of the lines and placed between them.

"Shoulder arms! Forward march!" The lines moved out of town into the cold rain.

Twenty minutes later there was a volley of shots. Feena shivered. Her mother pressed her hand, and with her other hand she crossed herself.

A few minutes later the same two boys were

back to borrow a shovel. It was returned cold and wet the same evening. The next morning the people of North Platte visited their tiny graveyard and counted sixteen fresh graves.

Rolling Belinda never rolled to Julesberg. It sat on the muddy main street as the other shabeens were taken apart or left to collapse under the spring rain. Nora and Feena sat in it.

They patched holes when it rained and sold Mr. Whiteleather's tea and sugar when someone asked for it.

By the time the excursion train arrived from the East, the grass was high on the prairie, the muddy streets were bone dry, and North Platte was clean.

The one hundred excursionists had been handpicked by Dr. Durant. Most were millionaires, able to invest one or two hundred thousand dollars apiece in a promising company like the Union Pacific. Some were celebrities: Robert Lincoln, son of the late President, had been invited, and the Marquis de Chambrun and the Earl of Arlie. A few reporters had been allowed to accompany the celebrities in the hope they would write a good story about the railroad. Finally there was Inspec-

*A few reporters had been allowed to
accompany the celebrities*

tor Boggs, who was there to certify that the new track was as straight and firm as it could be. For every mile of track laid on the prairie the government paid the Union Pacific $16,000.

For his excursion to the West, Dr. Durant wore a flat black hat, a flowing pink tie, and a velvet coat. His gray-checked trousers were cut in the French style. He walked up the dusty main street of North Platte in shiny black shoes. Beside him walked Inspector Boggs in a wrinkled black suit, and the Earl of Arlie in a plaid hunting outfit. An English servant followed with a basket of dirty clothes.

"You'll see, my friends, that the West does not quite live up to the picture of it that has been painted in the Eastern press." Durant motioned to the silent street. "No Indians on the rampage, no highwaymen terrifying the traveler, no gamblers robbing the honest citizen."

He knocked on the door of *Rolling Belinda*.

"Here, I understand, a respectable woman maintains a shop in perfect safety. Some day this may be a large business, supplying farmers within a radius of twenty miles."

"Farmers? I haven't seen any farmers along this part of the track," observed the Earl.

"They are coming every day, like locusts. They will cover every inch." At that moment Feena opened the door.

"Does your mother take in laundry?" asked the earl.

Feena blinked twice and said, "Yes, sir."

"It must be ready tomorrow. What time will we be passing on our way back East, Doctor?"

"At two-thirty in the afternoon, if we maintain our present schedule."

"Tell me, little girl," Inspector Boggs interrupted. "Who owns this building?" He tapped the flimsy wall with his cane.

"It belongs to Mr. Whiteleather," said Feena.

"And where is he?"

"Oh, he was shot with the gamblers," said Feena.

"Tssh, tssh, there isn't any shooting," interrupted Dr. Durant. "Shooting is a thing of the past. You never see any Indians around here, do you, child?"

"No," said Feena. "But they stopped our train." Dr. Durant coughed nervously.

"They stopped your train?" repeated Inspector Boggs. "I didn't hear about any trains being stopped."

"Yes, and then they burned it up," Feena went on.

"And why weren't you burned up too?"

"Because my brother ran through the snow with an Indian chasing him and got the soldiers to save us."

Dr. Durant cut in with a short laugh. "That's a typical western tall story, Arlie." He pinched Feena's cheek and added, "You mustn't make jokes in front of Inspector Boggs. He might take you seriously." He turned. "Shall we go? I wish I could offer you a chance to hunt Indians, Arlie, but they're a vanishing race. The Pawnee tribe eats from our hand already. Last year, land here was worth two dollars an acre. Now it's worth two dollars a foot. This has been made possible by the Union Pacific. The money that was made by the Pony Express, the Overland Stage, and the Cape Horn clippers—it will be ours. Invest now, my lord, and you will double your money in five years. . . ."

The threesome walked back down the street toward the waiting train. The English servant hung back. "Are there really Indians?" he whispered.

Feena nodded gravely. "Millions of them."

"That's beastly," he said. "I wish this whole rattletrap train was turned around and banging back to New York City. Tonight we have to sleep out on the prairie again and listen to speeches." The train hooted. The Englishman dumped the basket of clothes at Feena's feet and ran off after his master.

That evening, the excursionists had supper on the prairie. They read a menu printed that afternoon on the train and chose among the following: *Soupe à la Tortue* (turtle soup) , *Foie de Veau en Papillotes* (veal liver in white dough) , *Aspèrges à l'Huile* (asparagus in olive oil) , *Gateau d'Amandes* (almond cake) , and some two dozen other delicacies.

After dinner, the voice of Dr. Durant floated serenely across the starched white tablecloths and the glimmering candelabra. "Today, ladies and gentlemen, you bathed in the crystal waters of the River Platte. You saw with your own eyes a feat which last year would have been called impossible: the laying of eight hundred feet of track in thirty minutes. . . ."

Mike listened from a distance. He had been sent by General Casement to help out the excursionists. He had just set up a tent, and now he was spreading a pile of hay under it.

". . . This afternoon many of you hunted that strange beast of the plains—the buffalo, guided by our diligent U.P. scouts. And now we are dining on that strange beast of the sea, the tortoise, brought fresh via rail from the Atlantic. . . ."

The English servant stuck his head out of the tent next to where Mike was working and demanded, "Make sure you knock all the stakes in properly." He ducked back in.

Dr. Durant went on, "Tomorrow we will locate a new city here in your honor. The election of mayor and city council is at nine A.M. At two P.M., we visit a prairie-dog town. At five o'clock you are invited to a concert by the excellent St. Joseph's band. . . ."

Mike noticed that two men were standing above him. He looked up and saw General Dodge and Red Leaf.

"Who does that tent belong to—the King of England?" asked Dodge.

"No, sir, the Earl of Arlie," answered Mike. "But he doesn't sleep here."

"Who does?"

"His valet and his secretary. The Earl sleeps in that big tent, all by himself."

"And what do the servants think of the U.P. railroad?"

"They think it's very long," said Mike, "and bumpy."

Dodge laughed. "How about the Earl? Is he buying any railroad bonds?"

Mike scratched his head. "I don't know. I heard him dictating a letter to his secretary. I only remember one thing. He said Dr. Durant had a voice like a bagpipe."

Dodge turned to Red Leaf. "English Lord says this: Dr. Durant is a big wind." Red Leaf nodded and grunted. The general and the Indian boy squatted beside Mike.

"You're the boy from the Plum Creek fight," said Dodge. "We can trust you, all right. Red Leaf and his friends want to put on a dance for the guests. But Dr. Durant says there's no room for it in the schedule. So they're going to do it anyway about four o'clock this morning. You understand?"

Mike grinned and nodded.

"What you have to do is make sure Dr. Durant doesn't shoot anybody." Dodge took a revolver from Red Leaf. "Do you know how to empty the chambers of a pistol? Let me show you."

In the background, Dr. Durant's voice droned on, describing how the Union Pacific would change the Western plains into a veritable gold-lined paradise.

That night the chef's third assistant, worn out by his work making *Tête de Buffalo à la Western*, gave Mike the job of staying up all night to keep the campfire going. The guests were in bed before midnight. A few servants stayed up trying to finish washing clothes in buckets. General Dodge said good night to Dr. Durant, who toured the camp briefly and then crawled into his tent. The moon rose, but only wolves and Indians were awake to see it. The wolves howled.

Mike crawled behind Dr. Durant's tent and unloosed a peg from the flap. He raised the flap and looked in. Dr. Durant's head was about two inches from Mike's hand. He was sleeping on a lace pillow.

Mike stuck his fingers under one side of the pillow and wormed them forward slowly. Dr.

Durant's head rose a fraction of an inch as Mike's hand advanced, searching for metal. Nothing. Mike started back very slowly.

Dr. Durant's servant coughed on the other side of the tent. The doctor's head did a flip-flop, and he started snoring. Mike waited, then wormed his hand under the other side of the pillow. His finger

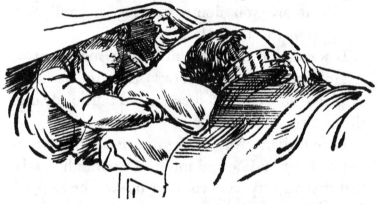

touched a cold object. Now his hand was around it. He started the long trip back, dragging the object over the matted grass. Fifteen minutes later, he emerged into the moonlight, holding a small pearl-handled revolver.

He opened it and dropped the six cartridges out, one by one. Then he pushed the revolver back under Dr. Durant's pillow, pegged the tent flap, and slipped back to the fire.

A couple of hours later Mike heard the sigh of a locomotive passing very slowly along the track. He went to Dodge's tent and shook him by the shoulder. "The Indians have arrived," he whispered.

On his way back to the fire, a white figure accosted him.

"What are you doing running around? Stay away from the tents, boy."

It was Durant, dressed in a white nightshirt.

Holding the little revolver stiffly in his hand, he glared at Mike, and then walked cautiously into the prairie.

Fifty Indians froze on the prairie as Dr. Durant stepped out and peered into the moonlight. Satisfied that all fifty were rocks or bushes, he stepped back. "Don't let the fire go out, boy," he said to Mike as he crawled back into his tent.

General Dodge joined Mike at the fire, waiting for Dr. Durant to go back to sleep.

As the moon sank, the first hint of dawn creased the eastern horizon.

At last Durant's resonant snore joined the whistling snores of two lady excursionists in the tent next to his. Dodge walked off quietly and Mike waited, listening. The only thing he could hear besides snoring was the wolves.

Then a shriek broke over the camp, followed by another and another. A swarm of grotesque red men were running through the tents. They howled and hooted, pranced and stamped at the tent flaps, slapped the canvas and plucked the ropes.

A lady, clutching her gown, ran toward the prairie and was rescued by General Dodge.

Inspector Boggs' tent collapsed. The Inspector wriggled inside it, waiting for a tomahawk to singe his brow.

Sleepyheads popped out of the tents and, sizing up the situation, quickly popped back in.

Dr. Durant was being chased by Red Leaf around his tent. "Get back, you devil," he warned, stumbling over his tent ropes.

Red Leaf took a tremendous swing at him with a tomahawk, carefully missing. Durant scrambled away and aimed his pistol. Click, click, click. Not one cartridge fired. The chase went on.

More ladies screamed.

A drum rolled. There was silence, except for

*Red Leaf took a tremendous swing at
Dr. Durant*

the sound of Inspector Boggs thrashing under canvas. General Dodge's voice sounded out like a bugle. "Good morning, ladies and gentlemen. You are invited to see the sunrise this morning in exactly eleven minutes. As an added spectacle, Troop "B" of the U. S. Pawnee regiment will perform an interesting tribal dance. Breakfast will be served in an hour."

The drum continued in a ragged beat, and as dawn broke, fifty perfectly tame Indians in outlandish war paint and feathers were seen dancing placidly around the campfire.

The English servant stepped up to Dr. Durant, who was looking sourly into the empty chambers of his revolver. "The Earl of Arlie sends his congratulations," he announced. "He says it was marvelous. Quite savage. Just like the West should be."

General Dodge and Mike helped Inspector Boggs out of the shambles of his collapsed tent. "Reminds me of Plum Creek, Mike," said Dodge. "You know the Sioux are camped only thirty miles to the north."

"You could have given us warning, General, before this savage display," said Boggs, crawling out of the canvas.

"Indians never give warning," said Dodge. "That's why our men get so nervous all along the line. They're not cowards, but they like to know that if they're attacked, someone will come help." He helped Boggs to his feet. "If you could mention to the right person in Washington that we need another five thousand troops between here and Fort Saunders—"

"I will, General. I will," said Inspector Boggs, pulling straws out of his hair in the pale, cold light of dawn.

CHAPTER EIGHT

At the Bridge

As a last spectacle, Dr. Durant had a prairie fire started for his guests. It crept through the tall grass toward the camp and then split into two scorching fronts. One turned east and swept behind the train as it rolled home. Antelope, prairie dogs, and buffalo were swept along with it.

The Eastern gentlemen quickly unpacked their sporting rifles and rushed back to the platform of the observation car. From there they could pot the game as it jumped across the track to safety.

Many days later the guests were still talking about this marvelous event—a hunt on wheels. The hunters thanked Dr. Durant and promised to buy Union Pacific bonds as soon as they returned to New York.

The other branch of the fire turned west and smoldered under the wind. Then the wind turned, and it became a wall of flame, walking over the prairie. It drove the animals across Lodgepole Creek, where many drowned. The flames burned themselves out along the bank. Only a little grove of trees continued to burn.

The bridge which Major Callahan was trying desperately to finish was only two miles from this grove. Sheamus Cullen had fallen in love with the land around it. The winding valley and tall trees were the first things he had seen in the West that reminded him of Ireland. He couldn't stop thinking that he should be there, building a farm for his family, rather than slaving on the bridge trestle one hundred feet above Lodgepole Creek.

"Cullen!" shouted Major Callahan. "Stop gawking. Get down to that cedar grove and cut me some piles before the whole thing goes up in flames. Take the little wagon with Murphy."

Mr. Cullen and Murphy, a half-witted man whom Callahan used for odd jobs, drove two miles along the riverbank and then walked into the grove. It made Sheamus Cullen sick to see the green branches wither and droop as the flames crept around the trunks. He and Murphy were chopping down two tall straight cedars when a voice interrupted them.

"Get away from those trees!" A stout woman, dripping wet and carrying a shotgun, was waddling toward them through the smoke.

"Who are you, shouting like a banshee?" Mike's father retorted. He was in no mood to be ordered about. The woman stopped. It was Widow Husker, wearing the same patched skirt she had worn on the river boat. The two looked at each other with teary eyes, coughing in the smoke.

"Those trees belong to me!" said the widow, raising her shotgun. Murphy started for the wagon.

"That's a lie," replied Sheamus. "The United States Government owns these trees and nobody else."

"It did until yesterday. Now they're sold." She pointed the gun at Sheamus Cullen's head. "One —two. . . ."

"What's the difference? They'll be ashes tomorrow." Sheamus whirled the axe over his shoulder and dug it into the trunk again. "Come back,

Murphy. She won't hurt you." He chopped at the trunk again and again, feeling the gun barrel following every move he made.

When he stopped for breath five minutes later, both Murphy and the widow were gone.

He chopped down two more trees and stripped them. He was sharpening his axe when he heard a chorus of coughing in the smoke. The widow's two sons appeared at the edge of the glade, holding axes. Then Mat, Shawn, and Patch were standing beside them.

"Go away, Sheamus Cullen, before we beat the starch out of you," said Mat. Sheamus turned red with fury. "This land belongs to me now. It's too bad you didn't join us in Omaha instead of worrying so much about Major Callahan."

"I'm going to him now, I am," answered Sheamus. "And I'm going to tell him where the three thieves are that broke their word to him." He swung into the cart, and Murphy drove off.

"April, May, June, July . . . ," Mike said to himself. It was four months since he'd seen his father. His knife flicked around the potato in his hand, and the peel fell into a knee-high pile. "I wonder if he's the foreman by now and can tell all the world how bridges should be built."

There was a hoot, and the cookhouse car, in which Mike was sitting, lurched forward. Mike tossed the last two potatoes into the corner so the cook wouldn't see that he hadn't finished. Then he chinned himself on the door, got a foothold on a handle, and scrambled out onto the roof of the moving train.

The telegraph operator passed a few yards away, shinning up a pole to cut down his lead wire. Carts and wagons passed above as the train snaked through a cut toward the river. Suddenly the bridge came into view. It was a beautiful, long framework that picked the track from one bank and carried it in a graceful arc to the other. Mike gasped with admiration. The locomotive jolted to a stop a few yards in front of the span.

A whistle sounded. The track layers were putting down their tools. Something was wrong.

Mike scrambled down to the ground and ran past the locomotive. Now he could see there was a gap about twenty feet wide in the middle of the bridge. Callahan's men were swarming around the gap like ants, dragging the final timbers into place and bolting them.

Callahan stood on the trestle holding a pocket watch in his hand and arguing with Casement. "But I have four-thirty. You'll be knocking off in a half-hour anyway."

"Three-thirty, you baboon. I saw you set your watch ahead an hour," said Casement. "We'd be a half-mile on the other side by now if your bridge were finished."

"She's finished! There she is!" cried Callahan. "What's an hour of work? In an hour you can roll right across. How about it, boys?"

"It might be an hour for a fast crew. But it'll take you and your farmers a day. No, Tim. I'm laying off. If you're lucky, Dodge will fine you for half a day only."

"That's five hundred dollars!" whispered Callahan. "Where am I going to get five hundred dollars?" And he followed Casement, clutching at his elbow and talking as fast as he could. No luck. In a moment he was back shouting orders. "Get that twelve by twelve into place. Drill another hole if that one don't fit! Come on, you ignorant blockhead. Come on!"

Mike looked everywhere, but he couldn't see his father. He sat down under the trestle, stuck a stalk of grass in his teeth, and waited.

A hundred feet ahead of him he could watch the men at work. They were tired. Some were just standing by, looking on. Others were bent double, straining to make the final connections around the gap.

Nothing seemed to go right. A man broke a bit drilling a bolt hole. Another let a timber slip; it narrowly missed the hand of a man working beneath him. Men cursed and grunted, grunted and cursed.

Mike suddenly realized that there was a world of difference between this and the quick, clean operation of Casement's track layers. Could bridge building be that much more difficult, he wondered.

Mike looked down and saw a cart pull up to the bridge's foundations carrying a lonely tree trunk in it. Two men got out. One walked with the clumsy movements of an idiot; the other man was Mike's father. The boy sat up, delighted, and watched.

The two men looked at the tree trunk for a while. Then they both tried pulling it out. Then one got into the cart and pushed while the other pulled. Then they changed around. Mike's heart sank. Could his father be just as clumsy and inept as everyone else working on the bridge? He watched in amazement as two voices sifted down to him from above.

"That's the contract: I have to pay Casement a thousand dollars for every day he's held up!" It was General Dodge.

"Shh, Grenville, you don't know what happened." Callahan was answering him. "That sand down there is a thousand feet deep."

"You mean your footing is no good? Then the bridge is no good!"

"It's good. But I had to build bins around the center piles and pour stone in."

"Four bins. How long could that take? When I saw you last week you promised me—"

"Casement's here a day early. You said we had to be finished by Tuesday."

"I said *Monday* or Tuesday."

"We couldn't work the men Sunday, you know."

"Don't blame your men for that. Get new men if they can't do the job working six days a week."

"I could do it working four days a week if they weren't listening all day long for an Indian war whoop."

"Blame yourself, Tim, or blame them. But this is your last contract with the U.P."

"But Grenville, I'm up to my ears already. You know what I lost at Plum Creek. All my material, my pile driver—"

"You better have this bridge finished by 6:00 A.M. if you don't want a second fine."

"I'll work them all night—"

"Listen, Tim," Dodge cut in, "what you need is teamwork, not sweat. If you're going to work tonight, you'd better take a break."

Callahan blew his whistle and the men stopped —all except Sheamus and Murphy, who were struggling up the side of the slope with the tree trunk.

"Is this what you're using—green wood?" asked Dodge, pointing to the trunk.

"No, no," said Callahan quickly. "This is for the bonfire. We'll need light to work by, tonight."

"Well, be careful you don't burn the bridge down while you're at it." Dodge walked away.

"Hurry up, Cullen!" shouted Callahan. And at that very moment Murphy slipped, and the tree trunk slid out of Sheamus Cullen's arms and bounded down the slope and into the river.

"Tarnation! You're a pair," cried Callahan, picking up a rock. "No wonder you were starving on the streets of New York when Ryan found you. I've never seen such a pair of imbeciles. Now get back to that grove and cut enough brushwood and small wood to keep a bonfire going here all night." He threw the rock into the river and walked off.

Sheamus Cullen found himself looking straight into his son's eyes.

"Hello, father," said Mike.

Mr. Cullen walked up the slope and sat down by Mike, wiping his brow. For a long time they said nothing.

"I'm working for General Jack," Mike started. "In the cookhouse. I make fifty cents a day." There was another silence. "I peel potatoes and things."

"Is it true the head of the U.P. started that prairie fire last week?" asked his father.

"He did," said Mike.

"I heard they herded the animals together and shot them and left the carcasses on the prairie. Is that true?"

"It is," said Mike.

"That's a sin, to waste what God gave us," said Mike's father. "God will curse the U.P. and all the men who work on the U.P. You remember what I'm telling you now. Something bad will happen this week, maybe today yet."

"Don't worry about that. How's the bridge coming?"

"Oh, we rush all day long with the bolts and timbers. The food isn't fit for a pig. And at night we listen to the Indians hooting in the hills."

"You'll soon be finished."

"And off building another bridge. I should be

down there in the valley, where it looks like a little piece of Ireland, building a farm instead."

"When the railroad's finished you will be."

"Did your mother get the money I sent her?"

"I don't know. I haven't seen her for months."

"We're all split apart now."

"Cullen!" Major Callahan's voice echoed between the steep banks. "If that fire isn't going by sundown, this is your last day of work."

"And now this!" said Mr. Cullen. "Burn precious wood all night because that man doesn't know how to build a proper bridge. It's a shame, I'm telling you."

Callahan's men went back to work at sunset. As the sky faded they crawled along the timbers around the gap. The bonfire blazed on the bank below, but its light flickered unevenly in the night wind. Lanterns were hung out along the trestle but with little effect. The men grappled with the clumsy timbers in the dark, straining to keep them in position, straining to force the bolts through. Their legs and arms ached already from a day of work.

When Mike returned, after peeling another thousand potatoes for breakfast, it was pitch black.

General Dodge was standing with Sheamus Cullen, watching the work. "Take care of this fire, Mike," he said, "so your father can help out. They'll be hoisting the connecting beam within the hour, Sheamus. They'll be needing a strong man like you."

"They need God's help more than mine," muttered Sheamus as he stumbled off over the uneven ground. Mike was shocked. He'd never heard his father talk that way to a man of authority. A few minutes later he heard his father's voice above that of Major Callahan's. "Give me that rope. . . . I have it, man. . . . Pull now."

The voices got more and more excited as the work neared its end. A man started singing an Irish ballad. Then there was a long hush. Mike's eyes strained to see what was going on over the river.

A cheer reached his ears. Then a voice crying, "Sheamus! Sheamus!!" And the sound of a body hitting the water below.

He darted down the bank. General Dodge was behind him. "To the left, Mike, that's the way the river flows."

"Father!" Mike shouted. "Father!" There was no answer. The black water stretched out for miles.

"That's far enough, Mike." Dodge plunged into the water. Mike plunged in too. It was warm and gurgly. He could see only the bonfire high above and a few beams under the lanterns.

"Father! Answer me!" Mike called.

They waded downstream, the water rushing around their waists. Dodge stopped. "I think we've missed him." He cupped his hands and called up at the lanterns. "Callahan, did you send your men along the banks?"

"Yeah-ess!" came the faint answer. They plunged ahead again, more slowly. Now they were directly under the lanterns. The huge wet piles glimmered faintly in the dark. The water was shoulder high.

"Shh," said Mike. He could hear someone breathing heavily in the water. He struck out into the channel, his heavy shoes sucking him down, paddling, paddling until his hand touched wood.

There was a hand stuck to the wood and an arm and a shoulder. A body hugged the pile, the head half sunken in water. It was shivering.

"Father?" said Mike.

"Don't touch me," whispered Sheamus through his shivers. "I've broken my back for sure."

CHAPTER NINE

The Decision at Great Salt Lake

As THE summer wore on, the color of the prairie changed from lush green to withered gray. The wind blew the dead grass flat, and the ground hardened. The iron rails, which had been too hot to touch at noon, now sent chills through the hands of the track layers. Still the men worked ahead up Lodgepole Creek into the Black Hills of Wyoming.

Flurries of snow swept the slopes. Indians in the hills stared not at the white man's iron road but at the heavy clouds that grew in the sky. Winter was coming.

The surveyors, the graders, and the bridgers came back through end of track. Still Casement's voice flicked men out of their bunks at dawn and worked them until early dark. On his huge map, the track showed as a thin, red double line. It inched from North Platte through Julesberg, Sidney, Cheyenne, until it was a thumb's width from Fort Saunders. That was as far as it got.

One evening snow started falling at dusk, and by dawn the next day ties, rails, barrels, tools, and the cook's dog, Gimlet, had all been buried under a white quilt of snow. They dug out Gimlet, Casement admitted defeat, and the boarding train returned to Cheyenne for the winter.

Sheamus Cullen's back, it appeared, was sprained, not broken. All through September, he lay in the shade of *Rolling Belinda,* staring at the sky. He had been in America a year, and he had plenty to think about as the muscles healed.

Feena did her best to keep him from sulking. She brought him a baby prairie dog that flopped around in a little box lined with hay. And in October, she propped him by the stove where he could chat with the dozen farmers who came to buy flour or sugar from Mr. Whiteleather's stock.

One day in November, while Mrs. Cullen was

off at a farm doing odd jobs, Mr. Cullen cleared his throat and said, "Isn't it a pity, Feena, that my name is Sheamus and not James?"

"Why don't you change it then?" said Feena, bringing him a coal to light his pipe, which had gone out.

"James. Jim. That's more American," said Sheamus, puffing at the dead pipe. Soon there were clouds of blue smoke around his face. He laughed. "I will. I'll be 'Jim' Cullen from now on." It was the first time Feena had heard him laugh in months.

General Dodge was away in Washington, elected representative from the state of Iowa. Before he left, he made sure Mike had a job in the locomotive shops at Cheyenne. The money Mike sent every Saturday was almost the only money the family saw all week.

Rumors came in January of 1868 that the Union Pacific Company was as penniless as the Cullen family. Work might not be continued in the spring. The men who sat by the barely hot stove with "Jim" Cullen, talked of going back East.

But in February, long trains carrying ties and rails passed on their way West. Somebody declared he'd seen the Lincoln car, now Dr. Durant's private car, rolling with them. Then rumors started that Durant had taken over Dodge's job and was making big changes in Cheyenne. The biggest news was that he'd selected Salt Lake City, over four hundred miles away, as the next winter base of the Union Pacific. Four hundred miles of track in eight months of work—that was more than any company had ever laid.

In March "Jim" Cullen got a letter from Mike saying he was being sent out by the Union Pacific on a survey party to Great Salt Lake to find the best line for the track. He mentioned also that Dr. Durant had given Major Callahan a contract to grade ten miles of line through the mountains.

When Feena finished reading the letter, her father got out of his chair, rubbed the small of his back with both hands, and declared, "Ask your mother to pack my work clothes. I'm going to Cheyenne on the afternoon train. That Callahan still owes me a week's pay."

"Twenty-one feet!"

Mike wrote down "21" on the chart.

"Sandy bottom!"

Mike wrote "S" next to the "21."

The little boat was supposed to be traveling straight west across Great Salt Lake, but waves were knocking it about badly. Two men were rowing, their oars slicing deep into the waves or skimming above them. Another man held the sounding line over the water. And the chief of the survey party, Mr. Reed, sat at the rudder and tried to steer.

"Twenty-three feet!" The linesman's words were whipped away by the wind.

"Twenty-three?" asked Mike, his pencil hovering above the chart.

"Twenty-three," repeated Mr. Reed. "It's not getting any shallower. Let's go back to shore before we get swamped."

Mike and the linesman got up, struggling to keep their balance, and reached for their oars. With four men rowing, the boat made a little better progress through the waves. Mike looked across the dark, foamy surface of the lake to where the sun hit the hills. The tents of another survey party were faintly visible. The Central Pacific's men were there. They too were looking for a line on which a track could be laid south of Great Salt Lake through Salt Lake City.

Two men were standing on the shore waiting for the boat. One was General Dodge.

"Greetings, Grenville," said Mr. Reed. "We thought they had you trussed to your seat in Congress."

"I escaped," said Dodge. "Meet Mr. Brigham Young. Mr. Young, this is Mr. Sam Reed, superintendent of construction for the Union Pacific." The two men shook hands.

Mike stood astonished. He had heard of Brigham Young, the Mormon leader who brought his people across a continent to found Salt Lake City. He had imagined him as a tall man dressed in long robes. Here was a short, stout man almost seventy years old, dressed like a prosperous farmer.

Young stamped the dry clay off his boots and smiled broadly in the afternoon sun. "I heard you were having trouble," he said to Reed in a loud, friendly voice, "finding the right path for the Union Pacific across the flats of Salt Lake."

"We've done six surveys," said Reed. "And none of them work out as well as the line north of the lake through Promontory Point."

"Last night," Young said with a twinkle, "I had a vision. The waters of Great Salt Lake rolled back and showed a highway running across the bottom. It was such a highway as the Hebrews used

when they escaped across the Red Sea from the wrath of the Egyptians. If you could find it, you would drive piles, would you not, and make a trestle clear from Salt Lake City to the other bank."

"Do you remember in your vision exactly where this road began?" asked Reed.

"No, I do not," said Young, smiling. "A vision shows us the truth of things but not exactly how to make that truth come to pass."

"I bet it began near that big rock that looks like a head," said Reed. Mike glanced at his chart.

Young turned where he was pointing. "I believe it did," he nodded.

"That's the deepest part of the whole lake, along there!" said Mike.

Young turned around. "You let this child contradict me?" he asked.

"It's not Mike who's contradicting you," said Dodge quickly. "It's the survey instruments."

"Look to your instruments, then," said Young, "to see if the devil is inside them."

"If we can find a line through Salt Lake City, we will come through Salt Lake City," said Dodge firmly. "If we cannot, we must miss Salt Lake City and go north through Ogden and Promontory Point."

Brigham Young walked to his horse, mounted, and announced, "If the Union Pacific does not come through Salt Lake City, you can expect no help from my people." And he rode off at a sharp trot toward the tents of the Central Pacific.

It didn't take General Dodge long to decide that there was no practical line south of Great Salt Lake.

The survey party packed up and turned toward its base in Salt Lake City. The twenty men and Mike realized as they rode back that they were probably out of a job.

In the next week General Dodge was threatened on three occasions by outraged townspeople who wanted the Union Pacific to pass through their city. Life became uncomfortable for the surveyors too. At the boarding house where they were staying, the food suddenly tasted horrible. The men took to eating their own ham and biscuits on the porch. They wondered why Dodge kept them in Salt Lake City at all.

Someone else was wondering about General Dodge's reasons too. One evening a stagecoach rattled up the street behind four sweating horses and halted in front of the boarding house. The door opened, and Dr. Durant stepped to the ground.

"Where's General Dodge?" demanded Durant.

"Sleeping, sir," Mike replied.

"Wake him up."

"He just came in from a long trip—"

"I just came in from Green River. Show me where he is, and I'll wake him up myself."

Mike took a lantern, led Dr. Durant up the narrow stairs, and opened the door to Dodge's room. Durant slipped off his gloves, stepped briskly to the bed, and nudged Dodge with his riding crop. Dodge's eyes opened. The two men looked at each other without speaking.

"Put down that lantern, Mike," said Dodge, "and open my map case."

"I hear, Dodge, that you have given Salt Lake City to the Central Pacific. You are most generous with things that don't belong to you."

"The Central Pacific doesn't want Salt Lake City because, Dr. Durant, it would cost fifteen or twenty million to fill in the lake and make a causeway."

"Nonsense! They can easily pass along the *south* bank to Salt Lake City."

"Perhaps so, but their chief engineer has recommended that his line, too, should pass *north* of the lake. Give me the map of Utah, Mike."

Dr. Durant paused and stroked his blond mustache. He had never thought of this possibility. "Why have you lost the friendship of Brigham Young at the very moment when we needed it most, General?"

"Brigham Young will have to make friends with us again for one reason. We'll get to Ogden *before* the Central Pacific. Then he'll have to deal with *us*—that is, if he wants rail service at all."

"When can you reach Ogden?"

"March first, provided the snow melts on time. I'm trying to get the Central Pacific to agree that the two tracks should meet some place north of the lake, say Promontory Point—"

"Promontory Point!" cried Durant. "Promontory Point! If the Union Pacific can't get at least as far as the Nevada border, we might as well give up." He touched the town of Humboldt Wells with his crop.

"Why?"

"I'll tell you why!" Durant muttered, slapping the bedstead. "Because the government pays us $48,000 and also gives us 12,800 acres for every mile we build in these mountains. Why do you always forget that fact, General?"

"Because I don't think we can beat the Central Pacific to the Nevada border," said Dodge very slowly. "Not unless we work through the snow."

"Then work through the snow!" cried Durant.

"That will add millions of dollars to your costs."

"How many millions exactly?"

Dodge paused and stared at the lantern flame for a long minute. "Ten million," he said.

Durant nodded. "It's worth it. We'll pick up five million in subsidies from the government plus lands worth at least ten million. You are an engineer, Dodge. You just don't understand business matters."

"Business is a gamble. I understand that much. If the C.P. decides to work through the winter too, you won't beat them into Nevada at all. You'll lose your gamble, *and* the ten million."

"I'll take that chance, General."

"You'll end up with two tracks going side by side, one the U.P. and one the C.P. That would be a waste, wouldn't it?"

"I'll take that chance."

"If the government sees two parallel tracks, I don't think it will grant a subsidy to either company."

"I'll take that chance also."

"Then you intend, Doctor, that the U.P. should lay track all the way to the West Coast?"

"Why not? You'd better get your survey party out immediately." Dr. Durant smiled. "Is that understood?"

"Yes."

"Good, General. I was afraid you'd lost your fighting spirit." Durant left the room.

Dodge lay down on his bed again and stared up

at the ceiling. "Tell the boys that we're surveying a line to the Pacific, Mike. They can count on another few months' work out of the U.P. Don't tell anyone that it's all a bluff. Understand?"

Mike nodded.

"You know the Chinese government wants me to build a railroad out of Shanghai, China. Suppose we give up the U.P., and you and I go work for them."

"Yes, sir!" said Mike, clicking his heels and coming to attention like a tin soldier. As he closed the door, he could hear Dodge chuckling softly to himself.

CHAPTER TEN

Playing with Dynamite

GENERAL DODGE'S tactics were right. The Central Pacific soon decided definitely to go north of Great Salt Lake. As soon as Brigham Young learned this, he made friends with Dodge again and told his people to help the Union Pacific in its race to Ogden.

The American public pricked up its ears at the news of a race. What happened in the hills of Wyoming, Utah, and Nevada, became front-page news all over the United States:

November 30, 1868. *Bloomfield Gazette*
TRACK LAID TODAY: Union Pacific—3 ½ miles.
     Weather in Wyoming: clear & very cold.
     Central Pacific—3 miles.
     Weather in Nevada: occasional snow.
DISTANCE BETWEEN TRACKS: 363 miles.

By this time, of course, everyone knew that the Union Pacific was planning to work through the winter. The Central Pacific announced that it, too, would keep working. Both companies turned to their backers to borrow millions more dollars.

The backers of the Union Pacific were horrified at the expense. They questioned Dr. Durant, who explained that it was due to the hardness of the ground in the wintertime. In order to make cuts and fills along the track grade, the ground had to be blasted, just as if it were rock. Dynamite was expensive.

The backers asked why the work couldn't be done in the summer, when the ground was soft. "Because the Central Pacific is racing across Nevada!" was the answer. "The Central Pacific will control traffic out of Salt Lake if we don't reach Ogden first. We must get that business ourselves!"

The backers were convinced.

In December, several Union Pacific grading teams could be observed strung out a hundred miles ahead of the track. They were pushing the grade westward across the desolate Utah slopes.

The breaths of the men were frosty white in the clear air. Some worked ahead, along the stakes, drilling into the slope where a slice of the hill had to be blown away. Some worked with sledge hammers to break big chunks of frozen dirt into smaller clods. Others shoveled these clods into place to smooth the grade.

The contractor for the first grading team was Tim Callahan. His new foreman in charge of making cuts was Mike's father.

One morning when Callahan's men came to work, they saw a strange sight. About one hundred feet above them a similar grading team was working, making the same kind of grade, exactly parallel to the Union Pacific stakes. The new grading team was headed not west but east! Not only that; it was made up entirely of Chinese.

"I thought the C.P. was supposed to be in Nevada still," said Jim Cullen, looking up at the figures in straw hats and blue linen pants busy above them.

"Jim, would you slip an extra stick of dynamite into this next charge for me?" whispered Callahan, winking.

"All right, Tim," Mr. Cullen whispered, winking back. They were on friendly terms at last.

"Lay off, boys," Jim shouted to the shovelers.

"That's good enough," he called to the drillers, who tossed their sledges down the slope and moved away, puffing warmth into their blue fingers.

"Stand back a good ways now." Jim picked six fat sticks of dynamite out of a box. "We're going to give the boys upstairs a little surprise."

He slipped two sticks into each hole and tamped them down with a pole. Then he dropped a fuse into each hole and tamped it in place, working slowly because of his bad back. All the while he was singing:

"Every morning at seven o'clock
There were twenty Paddies working at the rock.
The boss comes along and says, 'Keep still
And come down heavy on the cast iron drill.' "

As the third fuse started with a hiss, he ran back.

"Drill, my Paddies, drill
Drill all day, no sugar in your tea,
Working on the U.P. railroad.
And drill! And blast! And fire!"

The earth shook, and huge hunks of dirt broke out of the slope in a deafening roar. On the grade above, the Chinese team dropped to the ground. The only figure that still stood on the skyline was a burly foreman with a flaming red beard.

"Give us warning, you Paddies," he shouted. "What are you trying to do, blow us to Kingdom Come?"

Callahan's men grinned to each other and went back to work.

They worked until daylight began to fail in the west. The Chinese were still hard at it above, and it seemed they had made more progress during the day than the Irish.

"Shall we say good-by to them, Jim?" asked Major Callahan.

"I think we should, Tim. I don't think they heard us properly when we said hello to them this morning."

"Put two extra sticks in for me," said the Major.

A few minutes later, there was another explosion on the slope. The furious foreman with the red beard bawled down at them, "You almost killed one of us that time." But the Irishmen were far away on their way to supper.

Supper in the cook tent was in three shifts. Jim Cullen sat in on all three, passing out free tobacco to the men. They were gloomy tonight because this was the eleventh week they had gone without pay.

"How can the Major pay us?" Jim said to a sullen man named Mulvaney, who talked about quitting. "The U.P. didn't pay him for the last grade we made. They can't pay him until the track is laid and the government pays them. Can't you understand that, man?"

"I know what Callahan says," muttered Mulvaney. "I just don't know if it's true."

"General Dodge himself didn't get paid for a

year and a half. Is he quitting?" Jim looked around the tent. "The Major's done all he can for us—raised our pay to a dollar fifty, give us free tobacco, free stamps to write home. What more should he do—print money for the U.P.? Now do

you want to come along with him or do you want to give the whole railroad over to the Chinese?"

Frank Mulvaney was silent. "I *am* going along with him, aren't I?" he finally said. "I'm going along, good as the rest of you."

"The Major will get his money as soon as the

track is laid, I'm telling you." Jim made his point again.

Outside, horses' hoofs could be heard and voices guiding a wagon in the dark.

"Over here. . . . Watch the tree. . . . Steady!"

"Visitors!" Jim exclaimed. "Maybe it's a survey party." The tent flap opened, and a tall, handsome boy stuck his head in and asked for a light. It was Mike.

"Mike!" his father shouted, giving him a bear hug. "I thought you'd be in California by now."

"We were until last week. They called us back. You're looking grand, Father."

"A plate of food," Jim commanded, "and a mug of tea for my boy! This is my boy, Mike. We'll put you to work here with a sledge hammer and a shovel."

"I'm willing," said Mike. "I don't have anything better waiting for me in Ogden."

"Sit down by the stove now and warm your bones. You'll hear the boys call me Jim. Don't be surprised. That's my *American* name—James Cullen."

"Mike can help toss the dynamite," said Mulvaney, laughing. "Your father has taken to blowing up the Chinese and their redheaded foreman."

"Redheaded foreman!" exclaimed Mike. "That must be Big Red Crump. He has a red beard."

"That's him all right."

"I met him last summer on the way through Nevada. What do you want to blow him up for?"

"It's not him we're blowing up. It's the C.P. Railroad," said Mulvaney.

"Mike, what do you hear from home?" his father interrupted.

Mike took a crumpled letter out of his pocket as Mr. Cullen explained, "Mike here is famous in Nebraska. Did you ever hear about how that boy ran five miles through a blizzard at Plum Creek with the Indians breathing down his back? That was my boy. Read me the letter, Mike."

"It's from Feena," said Mike.

"My daughter," explained Jim. "She nursed me like a child when I was flat on my bad back."

"She has something to say about that," said Mike, as his finger looked for the line. "She says, 'If you see Father out there in the mountains, tell him to be careful. He will lift a heavy thing without thinking. I have seen him do it. He will hurt himself again, like on the bridge. Mother says he is too stubborn to listen to us, so you must tell him!" The men laughed, Jim Cullen louder than the rest.

"Yes, indeed," he said, "I can remember that night at Lodgepole Creek when I slipped into the water. I was the greenest greenhorn that ever came from the green shores of Ireland. I was worried more about wasting the lumber than getting the bridge built. All I could think about was getting my two feet onto a farm, but I didn't even have a good grip on the timbers where I was working! That was a while back—about seven hundred miles back, to be exact. Well, Mike, tell us the news from Nevada, if that's where you're coming from."

"It is," said Mike, as the cook set a plate of stew in front of him. "The news is the C.P. has got President Johnson's ear. They're telling him the U.P. is built so bad it's not fit for a switching engine, much less first-class passenger service. Yesterday morning the President ordered the U.P. to stop work where end of track is now, fifty miles the other side of Ogden."

"What does that mean?" asked Jim.

Mike picked up a knife and fork. "This grade

you're making will never carry any track on it. That's what it means."

There was a stunned silence as Mike started to eat.

By the time the Irish got out to the grade the next morning, the Chinese were already at work. The cold seemed to press down harder than ever. The men were sullen. After Mike's news nothing had been able to cheer them up—not even a fifty-cent raise offered by Major Callahan. They looked forward to one thing only—some fun with the dynamite that afternoon.

Mike called his father away from where the drillers were hammering.

"Father, I want to go back to Ogden," the boy said. His father was flabbergasted. "I think I can get a job surveying the rail link from Salt Lake City to Ogden." He looked over his shoulder. The survey party was leaving.

"But I just arranged with the Major for you to work here," his father said.

"I don't like that stuff," Mike said, pointing to a newly opened box of dynamite. "I'm afraid you'll get hurt again."

"Faith, it's the safest thing in the world."

"Let me meet you the day the tracks join, where-ever that'll be," Mike pleaded.

"I'm not going to tell you what to do, Mike. You're a big boy now."

"The wagon's waiting for me," Mike said apologetically.

"Run then," Jim Cullen cried loudly to cover up his disappointment. "Run ahead!"

Mike was already running behind the provisions wagon. His friends reached down and pulled him on board.

Jim watched the line of horses move out over the clay wastes. "See you where the tracks join," he shouted.

There was a stunning noise behind him. He turned in time to see a slice of earth peel off the side of the slope and fall over the drillers in the exact place where he had been standing.

The Chinese and Big Red were looking down the slope, laughing and pointing at the boulders that were leaping toward the Irishmen.

When the echo faded a voice shouted out: "Quick, your shovels, boys! Poor Mulvaney and Pratt are buried alive for sure."

CHAPTER ELEVEN

The Meeting of the Rails

THE closer the U.P. got to its goal, the greater its troubles grew. The government threw its support behind the Central Pacific and withheld money that it owed the Union Pacific.

From his paneled office in New York, Dr. Durant fought back at the government. He found new investors. He made friends in the Senate and pushed the work forward.

General Dodge made good his promise. With the rival railroad less than two hundred miles to the west, he pushed the U.P. track into Ogden early in March. The Union Pacific had won control of the whole Salt Lake Valley!

The same day the government again ordered the Union Pacific to halt operations. Inspectors were posted in Ogden with orders to report if the company dared lay one more foot of track.

There was no more money in the Union Pacific's treasury. Durant was confident, however, that he could hold off his creditors until the track was completed. He ordered Dodge to push the track ahead as planned toward the Nevada border.

The next day President Johnson struck back. He approved a loan of one and a half million dollars to the Central Pacific. This loan was to build track that would run right over the grade made by the Union Pacific graders.

It seemed that Dr. Durant must surely be defeated now.

But luckily for him, it was President Johnson's last day in office. The next day, an old friend of Dodge's became President—General Ulysses S. Grant. He ordered the million and a half dollars frozen until the affairs of both companies were investigated.

Dr. Durant breathed easier. He quickly accepted a compromise offered by the Central Pacific: the two lines would meet at Promontory

Point—exactly as General Dodge had suggested long before.

Congress accepted this compromise in April. At the same time Grant advised the Union Pacific to change its business practices. In particular, he said, the company should get rid of Dr. Durant.

But Durant was not going to stop now. The track was going ahead nicely at a rate of four, five, and even six miles a day. Dr. Durant ordered the Lincoln car for May 1 to take him and his friends west to celebrate the meeting of the rails.

The meeting of the rails! The idea filled him with pride in his accomplishment. He closed his desk on an unanswered telegram:

COMPLETION OF ROAD THROWING THOUSANDS OUT OF WORK. CALLAHAN, MC CURDY, AND OTHER CON-TRACTORS HAVE CLOSED OFFICES WITHOUT PAYING MEN. MUCH UNREST IN GREEN RIVER. ADVISE YOU PAY ALL OUTSTANDING BILLS POSSIBLE.

GRENVILLE DODGE

Four days later the Lincoln car was rolling into Green River, where a sullen crowd gathered to meet it. But the engineer had orders to keep his throttle wide open, and the train passed them by at full speed.

West of the town another crowd was waiting for Dr. Durant. The men stood in the middle of the track armed with shotguns. They halted the train, uncoupled the Lincoln car, and rolled it onto a siding. For two days it sat there as the telegraph wires hummed overhead.

First the men wired Boston and demanded their pay. Boston quickly informed Dodge that Durant had been kidnapped. Dodge wired the Army for troops, but the telegram was killed by an operator somewhere along the way.

The strike threatened to spread. Dodge wired Boston for cash. The next day a small black locomotive puffed up to the train and unloaded three small trunks.

Dr. Durant was relieved to see the three small trunks. He stood at a table in front of a portrait of Honest Abe Lincoln and paid out $200,000 to three hundred men.

Jim Cullen received $305.50.

On the morning of May 10, Mike caught a train out of Ogden. He looked through all the cars for his father. The passengers were mostly all sightseers bound for end of track to witness the meeting of the rails.

A couple of hours later the train stopped in a dismal valley, desolate except for a few stunted trees and some ramshackle huts. Here—1,086 miles from Omaha—the Union Pacific Railroad ended for good.

Mike got off the train and walked up to the locomotive. A few yards beyond it another track swept in from the mountains and stopped. That was the Central Pacific, winding 690 miles from Sacramento.

In the gap between the two tracks a lonely figure was squatting, picking up stones. It was Phelan. The side of his head had healed nicely.

"Phelan!" said Mike. "Did you see my father? You know, Jim Cullen—Sheamus Cullen."

Phelan didn't look up. His hand went on picking up stones and dropping them. "It's a big day," he said, staring at Mike's feet.

And it was a big day. Twenty thousand men had worked to bridge the continent. They had done it at least five years ahead of schedule. Thirty-nine million Americans had watched them do it.

Mike went from shack to shack. Men who had worked together for four years talked quietly, preparing to say good-by. Others punched and hugged each other. Nobody had seen Jim Cullen.

With a triumphant hoot, a Central Pacific train pulled up to the gap, and a half dozen men in long coats and carefully brushed hats got out. They were the officials of the Central Pacific. A cheer went up from the men who rushed out to meet them.

A hundred sightseers from the West Coast poured out of the train. They wanted to cheer something too, so they cheered for the cheering workmen. Soon the crowd was rocking back and forth, easterners and westerners singing and embracing each other.

Mike still couldn't see his father anywhere. Governor Stanford of California got up on a locomotive to speak. On the edge of the crowd a lanky man set a curious mahogany box on an oak tripod. It was a photographer who had come all the way from Omaha to record the historic event.

General Dodge said a few words after Governor Stanford. Mike continued to worm his way through the crowd, looking at every face. Behind Dodge sat a telegraph operator, holding his instrument on a wooden crate and tapping out a description of what was happening. His words passed like lightning down the wires that shot away toward Sacramento and San Francisco, toward Omaha, Chicago, New York, and Boston. Here, there were only a few hundred men gathered in the wilderness. There, there were enormous crowds waiting for word that the United States had finally been bridged by rail.

When Dodge finished talking, the operator sent out: "HATS OFF." From Maine to Texas, hats, caps, bowlers, and sombreros came off.

Sam Reed of the U.P. and Strobridge of the C.P. carried the last tie into place. It was made out of California laurel, highly polished, and bore a silver plaque with the names of the officers and directors of both companies.

An Irish team picked up a rail and bridged the gap on one side. A Chinese team in clean blue jackets and pants carried up another rail. Just as they were about to set it down, Strobridge halted them.

"Wait," he said. He waved away some of the crowd that was standing to one side and signaled to the photographer, crouched behind his black muslin. "Shoot!" he shouted.

The Chinese dropped the rail and ran. It took five minutes before Strobridge could coax them back, explaining that the mahagony box shot not bullets but photographs.

When both rails were in place, men swarmed over them with sledges, driving spikes down into every tie except the one with the plaque.

The Reverend Todd offered a prayer.

Dr. Durant and Governor Stanford approached the tie and set four spikes in place—two silver and two gold.

The crowd became silent. The operator sent: "ALL READY NOW," and crowds from Sacramento to Boston became silent too, waiting.

The silver hammer fell on the gold spike, once, twice, three times. "Tap . . . tap . . . tap," whispered the telegraph key—the signal for dozens of raised arms to pull dozens of bell ropes and start bells ringing from coast to coast.

The two locomotives moved up until they touched, and as the firemen reached across the gap to shake hands, a bottle of champagne was poured foaming on the rail beneath them.

Everybody cheered and threw their hats into the air. Their shouts echoed across the valley:

"Hurrah! Hurrah!"

In the midst of a cheer Mike found himself looking into Phelan's pale, empty face.

"Do you think this one has any gold in it?" he asked, handing Mike a rock.

Mike looked at the yellow and red streaks running through the rock. "No, that's not gold, Phelan."

"The man says there's a rock with gold in it," said Phelan.

"What man?"

"The man talking to your father."

"Where is he, my father?"

Phelan walked away. "I'm not supposed to tell anyone," he said. Mike followed him out of the crowd to a shack where a pony was tethered. Behind it, Jim was sitting on one side of a crate. An old man sat on the other side, his leathery face fringed with a dusty gray beard.

"I told you not to bring nobody here!" snapped the old man, folding up a map with long, wiry fingers.

"It's my son," Jim explained in a whisper.

"Can he keep a secret?" the old man asked.

"Better than I can. Mike, come ahead. How are you, boy? This is Pete Pottuck. Sit down."

"Thank heavens I found you," said Mike. "Mother and Feena have been waiting for us at Lodgepole Creek for a week." He turned to Pottuck. "We're going to buy a farm and settle down."

Pottuck and his father started laughing. They slapped their knees. Jim threw his hat in the air and caught it. "There's been a change in the schedule, Mike. Show him that Indian thing, Pete."

Pottuck took a yellow amulet out of a tiny

leather pouch and held it out in his calloused palm. It was shaped like an eagle's head and had a hole in it for a leather thong to pass through.

"What do you 'spect that is, son?" asked Pottuck.

"Gold?" guessed Mike.

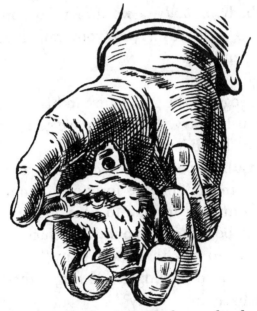

"Let *me* see," pleaded Phelan, who had been squatting on the ground nearby.

"Shoo!" said Pottuck. Phelan put his finger in his mouth and sat down again.

"No more farming, Mike," said Jim Cullen confidentially. "From now on I'm in business with Pete. Pete knows where that gold comes from. He's the only white man the Indians will let touch it. He's going to bring it out, and I'm going to sell it."

"We split fair and square—fifty-fifty. But don't tell nobody, *nobody*, a word of this. Don't want to start a gold rush. Just your father and me. Right, Jim?"

"Right, Pete!"

Mike joggled the gold figure in his hand. It was marvelously heavy. "Where are we going to live?" he asked, bewildered.

Jim Cullen took out a wad of bills and started counting them. "There's forty or fifty dollars left here I want you to take to your mother."

"How about the third pony?" Pottuck reminded him. "Got to buy that third pony."

Jim snapped his fingers. "I forgot that! Mike, do you have any money?"

"Two hundred dollars," said Mike. "You told me to save it for the farm."

"I know, Mike, but soon we're going to be rich, and we won't be needing a farm. You give that money to your mother to live on until Pete brings the first load of gold out."

Mike's stomach turned upside down. He'd worked hard for his money, and he didn't want to part with it. Suddenly he remembered a story about a confidence man who sold fake stock in imaginary gold mines.

"Ain't you happy you're going to be rich?" Pottuck asked, sensing Mike's disappointment.

"Sure," answered Mike. He tapped the eagle on the wooden crate.

"He don't understand nothing. Should never have told him, even. Give me back that amulet, boy."

Mike's fist closed around the gold. He wanted desperately to prove it was fake. "My father should keep it while you're gone," he blurted out.

"Mike's right," said his father. "I paid two hundred and fifty dollars into this business. I can keep the little eagle anyway."

"I told you I have to give it back to Chief Thunder Cloud," snapped Pottuck. "He'd take my scalp if I didn't bring it back to him."

"Take your scalp!" sang Phelan from a safe distance. "Take your scalp!"

Pottuck's hand fell on Mike's. "Should know better than to talk business with an idiot and a kid listening." Mike's blood rose in his cheeks.

"You don't have to talk to my son that way," Jim growled. "Mike, give him back the thing for Chief Thunder Bird, or whatever his name is."

Mike struck the eagle against a rusty nail and jumped up. Pottuck howled and flung himself at

Mike's arm as it shot up into the air. The sun caught the lump of gold. "Look!" Mike shouted.

There was a silver gash in the eagle's beak.

Pottuck stopped dead. "Silver!" he whispered. "There's silver inside! Silver and gold in the same hills."

Jim Cullen seized the eagle. "Silver? That's lead in there!" he hissed. He and Mike grabbed Pottuck with a single motion and started shaking him.

"Get up that $250. Get it up," Jim shouted.

Suddenly they realized Pottuck was laughing. They stopped shaking him. "Fifty years in the hills, and I finally got cheated by an Indian!" he was saying between bursts of laughter. "Gave me a lead amulet. I'm sorry, gentlemen. You can take all that's left. Strip me bare." He pulled out a mud-crusted wallet with a few crumpled bills inside it.

"We'll strip you bare, all right," Jim muttered. He ripped off Pottuck's coat and slit it open with his knife. Mike pulled the saddle bags off the pony and threw the contents across the ground. The old man screeched and cursed. Phelan laughed and rolled in the new grass.

In a hollow pick handle Mike found Pottuck's real gold mine—over $2,000 in greenbacks.

His father peeled off $250, stuffed a handful of bills into Phelan's pocket and threw the rest into the air. "Better pack up quick," he said, "before any other poor sucker hears you're in town. Come on, Mike. We're going home."

That same afternoon the gold and silver spikes

were pulled out of the laurel tie, and an ordinary tie was put in its place. Within a half hour, nothing was left of it. The sightseers had hacked it apart for souvenirs.

A third tie was being hacked to pieces as the bell on the roof of Promontory Station began to ring. A train was moving east.

It passed the car in which the officers of the U.P. and the C.P. were enjoying lunch together. It picked up speed opposite the squat shacks and the boarding train. It was carrying Mike back to a sister and mother he hadn't seen in two and a half years. It was carrying Jim Cullen to his old dream —a farm of his own.

CHAPTER TWELVE

A Home in America

WIDOW HUSKER sat outside her sod hut grinding hominy into flour. She rocked back and forth as the seeds popped and cracked. Her eyes watched the Cullen family in the distance.

Jim Cullen had driven their cart first to Sean's hut on the other side of Lodgepole Creek. They had stopped to talk to Mat where he was plowing in the May morning sun. At the ford in the creek they had risked crossing and now they were jouncing over a plowed field to the Widow's door.

Mr. Cullen gave the reins to Nora and jumped to the ground. "I don't suppose you'd want to sell part of your land," he said to the woman.

"Anything's for sale if the price is right," Widow Husker answered.

"I'm looking for land by the river, with a tree or two on it."

"Plant your own trees back there." She jerked her finger over her shoulder. "Get one hundred and sixty acres free from the government and make a forest." Jim turned to go. "Can't you take a joke? If you sit down on that bucket for a minute, maybe I can help you out."

Jim sat down and waited for her to talk.

In the wagon Feena was telling Mike about her garden.

"I had cabbages—two rows of them, big bushy ones—and sweet carrots and potatoes."

"You grew potatoes!" Mike's eyes opened. He felt his sister could do anything now.

"Yes, fat, white potatoes like in Ireland, and turnips, and what else did I have, Mom?"

"You had a tulip."

"But it died. And I had columbine."

"What's that?" asked Mike.

"Columbine—like there." She pointed to the walls of the sod house, which were thick with flowers—larkspur, phlox, and the first white and amber blooms of columbine. "Did you ever live in a sod house?"

"No, but I lived in a tent. And a train. And a hotel in Salt Lake City—"

"A hotel! Did you hear that, Mom? Mike lived in a hotel. Tell us about it."

Their father returned to the cart. "What's the world coming to anyway? She's willing to sell the whole farm."

"Are you going to buy it?" asked Nora.

"She wants $1500," said Jim. "She'll have to come down." As if to prove him right, the Widow's voice reached them, demanding peevishly that Jim Cullen walk around the farm and talk some more.

Mike and Feena went on chattering like two magpies. In a half hour their father came back and climbed into the cart. "She's come down to $1200," he whispered, snapping the reins.

The Widow put her hands on the horse's bridle. "You're not very friendly, are you?" she said angrily. "How much cash do you have, Jim Cullen?"

"Five hundred dollars," said Jim.

"Come on in the house. You, too, Mrs. Cullen. I'll give you a cup of tea." And she literally pulled Nora Cullen out of the wagon. "Did you ever see a sod hut with a wood floor? Well, that's what I have. A real pine floor."

Jim gave Mike the reins. "Drive around the farm," he said winking. "See if it's all there." Then he picked up a clod of dirt and strode toward the house, crumbling it between his fingers.

An hour later Mike was reporting to his father about how many acres had been planted. A scribbled agreement lay on the table between his father and the Widow.

"It's all swampy by the river," Feena interrupted. "And on the hill, it's all slate."

"Are you a surveyor, little girl?" challenged the Widow. "There's still a hundred good acres of good farm land, however you count them."

"And we found these," said Feena, opening her hand. There were a half dozen dried grasshoppers inside. "Hundreds of them, in the corn bin."

"Grasshoppers!" exclaimed Jim. "You were hit by grasshoppers last year! Don't tell me different, woman. I saw them in Wyoming. Clouds of them. So thick you couldn't see the sun! And five minutes after they landed on the crops, there wasn't a stalk left."

The Widow struggled to get a word in edgewise.

"No wonder you want to sell your farm!" shouted Jim. He pinched Feena's neck as he passed behind her chair, to thank her for finding the grasshoppers.

"Michael, you'll have to change that again!" And he tore up the agreement.

When the agreement was finally settled and the Widow and her son drove away, it was late. Mrs. Cullen asked where they were going. They talked vaguely about California. Farming was better there, the Widow said. She looked old and tired in the slanting red sunlight as her son turned their wagon toward the west.

Mrs. Cullen called after them to ask them to spend the night, but the Widow wanted to reach her older son's farm before dark. It was to him that Mr. Cullen would have to pay another five hundred dollars over the next five years.

"She can't wait to get out of here," Jim Cullen

chuckled, pulling off his boots. "I wonder if there's a curse on the farm."

"Hush!" his wife said. "Don't say that."

"What if there is?" said Mr. Cullen. "I can always sell the land like she did and go back to working on the railroad."

"Shhh," said Feena softly. "This is our home now." She put her arms around her father's neck.

"Look!" Mike exclaimed, running in with a warm, white hen's egg. "I found a chicken. You bought us the best farm between Omaha and Salt Lake." And he put his arms around his father and Feena at the same time.

Later that night after a supper of hominy cakes, turnips, and fried ham, Mrs. Cullen unfolded for the hundredth time a letter from Jim Cullen's brother in Ireland. Mike sat beside the flickering candle, his sister looking over his shoulder, and read it aloud:

Dear Sheamus:

Nora wrote me of your great good luck in the New World what with working on the railroad for a dollar and fifty cents a day which is according to Bartley Byrne here more than eight shillings. May St. Christopher protect you always in your journey. Father Malone said mass for your Peter a week ago Easter, and he is remembered here also in our hearts when Bridgit and myself pray for those who have left Ardrahan. There is a new manager demands the rent money week of Michaelmas or lose all to the landlord. Many more are leaving for America. The black mare is gone lame and I cannot plow. If you could spare 25 shillings I would buy a strong horse and sell the calf when the cow foals and pay you back before autumn.

> *Your brother,*
> *Patrick Cullen*

"It's that manager pushing him," said Nora bitterly. "You must send him the 25 shillings."

"No," said Jim. "He's paid enough to the manager. What use is it to send good money after bad? To my way of thinking he should pack up and bring Bridgit and the children to America."

"Here?" asked Feena, astonished at the thought.

"Why not?" said her father, his eyes bright with excitement.

"In this house?" asked Nora Cullen, looking at the sod walls surrounding them.

"Not in this house, in their own house. If that old widow woman could set up Mat and Patch and Sean, I guess I can set up my own brother on the land behind us."

"But the money!" Mrs. Cullen exclaimed, suddenly terrified of the idea. "Are we millionaires all of a sudden just because we're sitting in a sod hut we half own?"

"Children, let your mother and me talk, and then, Michael, you can write down the thoughts I want to send your uncle. Pinch the candle on your way out. We must save every penny now."

Mike and Feena felt their way to the door. Outside, the moon poured light across the fields. The air was alive with the sound of crickets. The ground under their feet was still warm.

They wandered toward the river. The grass on the banks was almost knee high already. Where the ground was soggy they climbed up through chokeberry bushes and wild grapevines to the fields again.

Before they knew it, they were within sight of the bridge.

"Where are we going?" cried Feena, caught in a bramble.

"Come on, I'll show you." Mike hurled a broken branch onto the black and silver water.

Mike ran ahead, whistling and hiding, until Feena found herself under the bridge. Mike was sitting on a rock tossing stones at a pile. Feena flopped down beside him, panting.

"Is this where Father was hurt?" she asked.

Mike pointed to the moonlit trestle above and then to the water. "Thirty-foot fall," he replied.

"And where were you?"

Mike pointed to the far bank. "Over there, with General Dodge. Don't tell anybody, but—" Mike paused.

"What?"

"You'll tell."

"No, I won't. Tell me!"

"Promise?" Feena promised.

"I'm going away."

"Where! You just got here! Don't go away!" Feena wailed. A frog jumped into the water.

"I'm going. You'll never guess where."

"Where?"

"China. General Dodge is going to build a railroad in China and he asked me to go too."

"When?"

"I don't know. He'll send for me." In the mid-

dle of the swollen current a fish leaped into the reflection of the moon and then sank back into blackness.

"You're fooling me," said Feena. She yanked a blade of grass out of the ground and looked at him.

"You *are* fooling, aren't you?" she whispered, tickling his nose with the blade of grass.

Mike broke into a giggle and ran up the bank, Feena hot after him.

"Don't you make any more jokes like that," she cried.

"Shh!" Mike said sharply. Feena's voice was still echoing across the water.

"Listen." There was a hollow sound in the distance. "Put your hand here." Feena put her hand against a pile. She could feel it trembling.

Across the moonlit prairie a freight train was approaching: a dozen boxcars, a dozen flatcars, and two passenger wagons with faintly lighted windows. It was an immigrant train—the same kind that had carried the Cullens from Omaha.

It thundered across the delicate silhouette of the bridge. The piles rocked and swayed until the whole structure seemed about to collapse. But it didn't.

"It's a good bridge," Mike said proudly, as the train passed off west.

"And you'll be staying right here with us?"

"I'll be staying. Where else would I be going? America's my country now. Come on. We have to get home to write the letter to Uncle Patrick."

"Home," echoed Feena.

They ran up the slope and across the plowed fields in a giggling, panting, galloping race for home.

About the Author

DAVID SHEPHERD has had an exciting and varied career as a teacher, theater-group leader, and writer. A native New Yorker educated in New England, Mr. Shepherd was introduced to Europe during World War II and remained in Paris to write. Since then he has taught composition to teen-agers in Bombay and playwriting to adults in Chicago and has founded a number of unique theater groups, including an informal theater in which the audience provided ideas from which the actors produced extemporaneous scenarios. In 1959, Mr. Shepherd returned to New York City where he now lives with his wife and their little boy.

About the Artist

WILLIAM K. PLUMMER lives in Pennsylvania Dutch country, where he and his artist wife work in a converted barn studio. Mr. Plummer is a graduate of the Philadelphia Museum School of Art and has been a member of the school's teaching staff for more than twelve years. A love for historical detail and accuracy has well prepared him for his specialty. In addition to book illustration, Mr. Plummer's work has appeared in such magazines as *Holiday*, *Esquire*, *Good Housekeeping*, and *American Heritage*.

About the Historical Consultant

JOSEF BERGER, a distinguished writer and journalist, was born in Denver, Colorado. A graduate of the University of Missouri School of Journalism, Mr. Berger is a crack newspaperman, novelist, and the author of many books for children. In addition, he has received a number of honors including the first prize in the *Atlantic Monthly* Essay Contest, the McAnaly Prize for Literary Composition, and a Guggenheim Fellowship. Josef Berger's articles have appeared in such magazines as *Atlantic Monthly*, *Esquire*, and *The New Yorker*.